PAUL FLEISCHMAN

SEEK

SIMON PULSE
NEW YORK   LONDON   TORONTO   SYDNEY   SINGAPORE

9-08   Book fair profits #08- 333   £ 7.00

FOR PATTY

First Simon Pulse edition March 2003

Text copyright © 2001 by Paul Fleischman
Published by arrangement with Carus Publishing Corporation

SIMON PULSE
An imprint of Simon & Schuster
Children's Publishing Division
1230 Avenue of the Americas
New York, NY 10020

Design by Anthony Jacobson

Printed in the United States of America
2 4 6 8 10 9 7 5 3 1

The Library of Congress has cataloged the hardcover edition as follows:
Fleischman, Paul.
          Seek / Paul Fleischman.—1st ed.
                    p. cm.
          Summary: Rob becomes obsessed with searching the airwaves for his long-gone father, a radio announcer.
ISBN 0-8126-4900-1 (cloth)
[1. Fathers and sons—Fiction. 2. Radio—Fiction.]   I. Title.
PZ7.F59918 Se 2001
[Fic]—dc21   2001028869

ISBN 0-689-85402-1 (Simon Pulse pbk.)

PRAISE AND AWARDS FOR PAUL FLEISCHMAN'S *SEEK*

SEEK

[We hear a wordless recording of wetland sound effects: frogs croaking, birds calling, water rippling gently. It has a night feel, soothing and mysterious. We hear a different portion of it each time it recurs, each featuring different sounds: an alligator's thrashing, a thunderstorm, a new avian soloist. It begins fading out after half a minute, overlapping the first few lines of dialogue.]

Rob
Remember in London, St. Paul's Cathedral?

Rob's Mother
Sure.

Rob's Grandmother
[reading]
"The elevator operator was a skinny redhead with more lipstick than lips. 'Well, Mr. Brindle,' she said.

'You're an early bird this morning.' He stubbed out his cigarette. 'I've got a date with a worm.' "

Rob
Remember climbing all those stairs to get up to the dome?

Rob's Grandfather
Boys your age, Robbie, working in the coal mines. Nine-year-old girls in the textile mills, some of them—

Opera Radio Host
After the overture, the curtain rises on a ball at the palace of the Duke of Mantua—

Rob
And remember, there was a walkway around the inside of the dome?

Rob's Mother
Sure I remember. The Whispering Gallery.

Aunt June
[reading]
"Slate-black except for white belly and outer tail feathers. Catches insects on wing, hunting from perch. Voice: a thin, strident *fee-bee, fee-bee.*"

1st Radio Announcer
This is HCJB, the voice of the Andes, broadcasting

from Quito, Ecuador, on the nineteen and twenty-five meter bands at fifteen-two-eight-five—

Rob

Remember how voices moved around the dome, so you could hear what someone was saying way across on the other side? And then that whole class of school kids came up—

Rob's Mother

All talking at once.

Spanish TV Actress

Te juro, mi vida. Con todo mi corazón, te amo!

Rob

That's what it's like. Exactly. Voices bouncing everywhere.

Mr. McCarthy
[reading]

"—will serve as your senior thesis in English. Like the autobiographies we've read this year, yours should probe the themes in your life, analyzing signal events and charting the influences of family, community, and your historical era on your development. All information will be treated as strictly confidential. On the brink of your departure from high school, this is a chance for you to look back and use both your literary and critical thinking skills—"

Rob

Ever since McCarthy gave us the assignment.

2nd Radio Announcer

Two on, two out. The Giants really need a hit here. Bonds waits, wagging his bat.

Rob

Except instead of looking back, it's like I keep . . . listening back.

[We hear the sound-effects recording. It begins fading out after half a minute, overlapping the following speech.]

Lenny

It's eleven o'clock at Oldies 93. Another Tuesday night, I'm Lenny Guidry, and it's request time. A little show we call "The Ghost Raising." Most appropriate at this time of year. Had us a bunch of ghosts and goblins at the door trick-or-treating last night. You know what trick-or-treating's really about? Making the dead one's favorite foods. That's what brings 'em back home. Down in Mexico, at Day of the Dead, they bring the meal right there to the cemetery. Now tell me—you know anybody whose favorite meal was five pounds of little bitty candy bars? Well, maybe some of you do. But for my old ones, I always make gumbo. So that's why I drove all over the whole Bay Area looking for okra, which put another hundred miles on Anne-Marie, who's already got three hundred thousand on her and arthritis in both axles, but you just can't make gumbo without okra. So I spend all day cooking it up, stirring the roux, got the chicken necks, everything, and who comes to the door? Not Aunt Bernadette. Not Aunt Camille. Not Uncle Gervaise—and that man did like gumbo, died right in a restaurant in Opelousas, Louisiana, with his napkin still tucked in his collar and a shrimp tail sticking out his mouth. Didn't none of 'em come. Somehow, don't ask me, that gumbo called a bunch of grabby, greedy, runny-nose little kids that I don't even know. And I'm just about sure not one of 'em was dead. . . . Now if that happens to you, and you want to see someone you're missing, you just call us up at 767-8900 and leave a message, talk as long as you want and tell me what you want to hear. 'Cause music works as good as food. Brings back the old times and the old folks. Makes your wallpaper change right there on the wall to what you had when you were a baby, or maybe to when you and your baby first met. So let's turn back the clock and raise a few ghosts. Maestro, the message machine.

1st Female Caller

[a teenager]

Yeah, my name's Tracy and I want you to play "Gotta Lotta Love" by Shriek and I want you to play it for Randy 'cause I miss him so much and he hasn't called me forever and we had such really, really fun times back then. Randy, I love you!

Lenny
Hold on a second. Such fun times "back then"? "Forever"? This song's about three weeks old! Whoa, Tracy. If that's way back in the past, I want to know what geologic era we were in when Nixon—

Rob's Grandfather
So the longshoremen decided to go on strike. They stopped loading and unloading ships and they blocked the docks with picket lines. You already know about the Fourth of July. But did they teach you in school about the *fifth* of July?

Rob
[reading]
"Autobiography of Robert A. Radkovitz. By Robert A. Radkovitz. Part One. Chapter One. Preface. . . . I grew up in a house built of voices."

Rob's Grandfather
The fifth of July is famous in San Francisco. It's called "Bloody Thursday," because that's when the big businessmen—

Boy Rob
Are they the bad guys?

Rob's Grandfather
Right. Very bad. So bad that they paid for scabs to

drive trucks right into the line of strikers, right down there at Pier 38.

Boy Rob
I have a scab. On my elbow. Look.

Rob's Grandfather
Grandpa sees. But this kind of scab is different. It's a man who doesn't belong to a union. Grandpa sees. Remember unions? They're like a team. Grandpa sees, Robbie. Put your arm down now.

Rob
[reading]
"—neither forgetful, sugar-sweet, nor marooned in an easy chair. My grandfather was and is a history professor at UC Berkeley, specializing in labor history. He may be the very first to attempt teaching it to a six-year-old."

Rob's Grandmother
[reading]
"'I shall be blunt,' Marston began. 'Something is rotten in Dorset. And the smell is coming from Hamberly Hall. They found the gardener's body this morning—throat slashed from John o'Groat's to Land's End. And Lady Emma, it may interest you to know, has not been taking painting lessons in London, but rather has been visiting a doctor tucked well out of view in Lambeth.' 'Good God! Abortion?'

'Worse,' Marston replied. He relit his pipe and exhaled. 'Syphilis.'"

Rob's Grandfather
Shirley—the kid's only in kindergarten.

Rob's Grandmother
Yes, dear, I know. But he so loves being read to.

Rob's Grandfather
He loves it? He's asleep!

Boy Rob
No I'm not.

Rob's Grandmother
You see.

Rob's Grandfather
Well, he oughta be. How's he supposed to keep the barristers separate from the solicitors, or understand why the rector's blackmailing the vicar? They don't get to blackmail and extortion till third grade.

Rob's Grandmother
The sense is for me. The *sound* of the language is what he's getting. And frankly, dear, I'd much rather he be exposed to the prose style of Agatha Christie than Karl Marx. Marx really had no ear for dialogue.

Rob
[reading]

"—and then read most of Dickens to me. Books are something I hear, courtesy of my grandmother. She's a vocal quick-change artist: narrator, chimney sweep, murderer, maid. Mysteries are her dessert. She reads constantly, and did so for a living: proofreader, newspaper copyeditor, then editor at several publishing houses. I've seen her read the dictionary for an hour. Whenever I look up a word, it's my grandmother's voice I've always heard in my head."

Rob's Grandmother
[reading]

"Pubis: That part of either innominate bone that, with the corresponding part of the other, forms the front of the pelvis."

Rob
[reading]

"Even if I didn't want to."

Rob's Mother

So what day is Jeremy's sleepover?

Boy Rob

Saturday.

Rob's Mother

Saturday? Darn! Grandma and I are going to

Siegfried at the opera house and we knew you'd want to go so we—

Boy Rob
Is that the one where the guy kills the dragon and when he tastes its blood he can understand birds? And there's that lady asleep with the fire all around her—

Rob's Mother
—and he has to walk through it.

[pause]

Boy Rob
Maybe Jeremy would want to go.

Rob
[reading]
"—since we've lived with my grandparents. I have no brothers or sisters. I was raised among adults and treated as one. It's as if they couldn't wait for me to catch up to them—to history and opera and politics and Lord Peter Wimsey—and so they didn't."

Rob's Mother
Good night, angel.

Boy Rob
No—in French.

Rob's Mother
Bonne nuit, mon ange.

Rob
[reading]
"—teaches high-school Spanish and French. She also speaks Italian and some German. Barn swallow is to air as her tongue is to language. When we go to the opera, my mother doesn't need to read the translation. She writes poetry and has kept a journal for more than twenty years. She belongs to a writer's group that meets once a month at our—"

Boy Rob
Now say "sweet dreams."

Rob's Mother
Fais de beaux rêves.

Rob
God, I used to love to look at your lips. It seemed so amazing that you could make those strange sounds with them.

Boy Rob
Just one more time.

Rob's Mother
Fais de beaux rêves.

Boy Rob
How do you do that?

Rob
[reading]
"My grandparents' house is a Victorian on Potrero Hill. It was divided vertically into a duplex before they bought it. When the last of a long line of deranged tenants left, my mother and I moved into the right side. I was a few months old. Since my grandparents helped take care of me when I was little, we put in a connecting door on the second floor for convenience. My mother preferred it closed, for privacy, but I liked all the different voices coming from—"

Exercise Video Voice
—keep it going, keep it going, this is gonna tone your quads *and* your glutes, so you're really killing two flabs with one—

3rd Radio Announcer
Coming up on KPFA, "Delano Diary," a radio portrait of the United Farm Workers' historic grape boycott and a look at its long-term—

Audiobook Reader
"It was half past five before Holmes returned. He was bright, eager, and in excellent spirits."

Spanish TV Actress
¡Maléfico! ¡No me digas mas!

Spanish TV Actor
Esmerelda, lo siento. Lo siento tanto. Es que, es que—

Spanish TV Actress
¡Canalla! ¡Déjame! ¡Este momento!

Boy Rob
What's happening?

Rob's Mother
She really wants him to leave.

Rob
[reading]
"Each person not only had a voice but brought others into the house: the voice of radio, of books on tape, of my mother's Mexican soap operas."

Spanish TV Actress
¡Maldito! ¡Mentiroso! ¡Eres un tipo de lo más bajo!

Boy Rob
Now what's happening?

Rob's Mother
She called him a liar and a scum.

Boy Rob
Why?

Rob's Mother
Well, sometimes, sweetheart, people do very bad things, even though they know they shouldn't.

Boy Rob
What did he do?

Rob's Mother
Well, he married two different women at the same time. This one, and that one in the very tight dress.

Boy Rob
He forgot?

Spanish TV Actress
¡Que los testículos se te asen en el infierno! ¡Y que las cabras orinen sobre tu tumba!

Rob's Mother
Not exactly.

Boy Rob
What did she just say?

Rob's Mother
That she hopes his testicles will roast in hell and that goats pee on his grave.

Rob
[reading]

"She watched them to keep up with current Spanish. I learned more from them than from health class, psychology class, and the dictionary combined."

Mr. McCarthy
[reading]

"—may wish to interview relatives or other significant figures in your life. Like authors before you, you can draw upon letters, journals, diaries, memorabilia—"

Rob's Grandmother
[reading]

"It was the best of times, it was the worst of times, it was the age of wisdom, it was the age of foolishness—"

Opera Radio Host

—singing the part of Zuniga this afternoon. And now Sven Talburg, our Escamillo, glittering in his sequined gold vest and tight pants, bounds onstage with a toreadorlike flourish and bows, receiving a very warm ovation. *And here comes our Don José—*

Rob's Grandfather
[reading]

"—this patently asinine view of free trade, so beloved by the well-heeled dimwits who bankroll your dismal newspaper—"

Rob
[reading]

"—the Saturday opera on the radio, my grandfather reading his never-published letters to the editor, the writer's group reading poems and stories, the Giants games I listened to in the evenings—"

4th Radio Announcer

I mean a *huge* gap between first and second. If Butler could manage to poke one through, and Thompson and Clark could somehow get on—

5th Radio Announcer

—that would bring the tying run to the plate.

Rob

"—the announcers openly rooting for the home team, concocting improbable comebacks, willing balls to stay fair or go foul—"

4th Radio Announcer

A lazy fly to center. GOO-tee-air-ez under it—

Rob's Mother

Goo-TYER-ez!

Rob
[reading]

"—and mercilessly mangling the Spanish surnames."

4th Radio Announcer

He squeezes it for out number two. That brings JIM-a-nez to the plate.

Rob's Mother

Hi-MAY-nez! Can you believe that? I swear I'm going to write a letter to the team.

Rob's Grandfather

A letter? Good luck, Rose! Here's a stamp. Be my guest!

Rob's Grandmother
[reading]

"—it was the season of Light, it was the season of Darkness—"

Female Writer

This is a little haiku I've been polishing for a couple of months, actually since last summer when I went to the Japanese tea garden. Or was it spring? The rhododendrons were in bloom, I recall. Quite lovely. Anyway, I'd be especially grateful for Rob's reaction, as the youngest member of the group. Because I think it's a subject that's really more likely to resonate with a—

Male Writer

A haiku has seventeen syllables, Marjorie. You've already used up a hundred and ninety.

Mrs. Kathos
Stand straight, Robbie, so I make the mark in right place. Now, let's see if you grown.

Rob
[reading]
"Outside the house, next door there were our old Greek neighbors, Mr. and Mrs. Kathos, who treated me like their own grandchild and overpaid me for the simplest chore with square after square of sweet baklava."

Rob's Grandfather
Let me get this straight. They're paying you with *pastry*? What the hell kind of wage is that?

Aunt June
"—two white wing bars, partial eye-ring." Robbie— that's it. A Hutton's vireo!

Rob
[reading]
"—my two wonderful aunts, my mother's sisters, neither of them with their own kids: June, the biologist who took me bird-watching, and Jessica, a teacher who knew boys love big trucks and who drove me on Saturdays to construction sites."

Aunt Jessica
Look—a grader!

Boy Rob

Wow!

Aunt Jessica

Man, it's huge! Check out that blade. We are *so lucky*!

Rob
[reading]

"Everybody wanted me. I was respected and courted and adored."

Rob's Mother, Grandparents, Aunts
[singing]

Happy Birthday to you,
Happy Birthday to you—

Rob
[reading]

"And yet I was dissatisfied. No matter how loudly they sang, I was aware that there was a voice missing from the chorus. My father's voice."

Rob's Grandmother
[reading]

"—it was the spring of hope, it was the winter of despair, we had everything before us, we had nothing before us—"

Rob
[reading]

"Somehow, that missing voice seemed to out-weigh all those that were present. By the time I was seven or eight, I'd made up my mind. I would find him."

Rob's Grandmother

Now make a wish.

Rob's Grandfather

Think about it.

Aunt Jessica

Take your time.

Rob's Mother

Don't tell anybody.

Aunt June

That was fast. The kid knows what he wants.

Rob's Grandparents

And look at him blow!

[We hear the sound-effects recording. It begins fading out after half a minute, overlapping the following speech.]

Lenny

By request, the Beatles doing "Yesterday" for another satisfied customer here on "The Ghost Raising." Lenny here till one A.M. *It's not always that easy, tracking down requests. Sometimes I spend a whole afternoon checking the used record shops or going through my Rolodex of experts who got their Ph.D.'s in early Delta blues or late Dean Martin. Like with this request here.*

2nd Female Caller
[an old woman]

I would kindly like for you to play for me the Mother Goose Suite *by Maurice Ravel, not the version for orchestra but for four-hand piano, two people playing, do you understand, which my cousin and I used to play together, sitting on the same bench. Both of us were quite serious about piano, we were the same age almost to the day, and since I had only brothers she was like a twin sister for me, until we were separated, you know, in the war, we both lived in Hamburg, the city of Brahms, my family got out in nineteen thirty-one, hers stayed, they couldn't get visas, you know, no one ever saw her again, or the rest of her family, and so, and so I didn't play this music again, I really couldn't, but now I am very old and I would like to hear it one more time and feel her beside me, but the people told me it's only on a CD, but I don't have a CD player, and if you could play it near the beginning of your show because it's difficult for me to stay awake so late I would be very, very appreciative, thank you.*

Lenny

Whoa. But that's what the show's about. It took some doing, put some more miles on Anne-Marie, but I finally found it, one piano, four hands. And tonight, violating

sacred AM radio law by playing anything longer than
three minutes, at peril of eternal excommunication from the
airwaves—but also knowing the station manager never
listens to the show—you're gonna hear all fifteen and a
half minutes of—

Rob's Mother

I remember holding you, a few hours after you were born. June was in the room. I was talking about Lenny. You woke from a nap and stared at me, and I stopped talking. I didn't want you to hear. I was so used to you being inside my body, but now you were out. And then the thought hit me: What had you overheard all those months just a room away, on the other side of the door?

Boy Rob
[reading]

"The capital of Louisiana is Baton Rouge. Its state flower is the magnolia. Its—"

Rob
[reading]

"I'm a night person. I was formerly a night boy, and before that a night baby. I was born at night— three twenty-two A.M. Night's my hometown, the place I'm comfortable. For me, the morning sun is like a loud drunk: obnoxious, unwanted, demanding attention. The sun is so bright it hides. The constellations are always there above us, but can only be seen after dark. Day-submerged sounds come out with the stars: crickets in the grass, a piano half a block away, the car-trailing-tin-cans clatter of a river heard from a cabin. Moths, the night's butterflies, emerge, pollinating the night-blooming flowers. And most important: radio waves travel farther at night."

Rob's Mother

We were so incredibly young, both of us. I was young, and he was younger. Remember "The Jumblies," the Edward Lear poem? When you were little, you could recite the—

Boy Rob

"They went to sea in a Sieve, they did,
In a Sieve they went to sea:"

Boy Rob and Rob

"In spite of all their friends could say,
On a winter's morn, on a stormy day—"

Rob's Mother

I'd hear those first words, and I'd think: That was us.

Boy Rob

"In a Sieve they went to sea!
And when the Sieve turned round and round—"

Rob

How old were you when you met?

Rob's Mother

I was twenty-five, just finishing my teaching credential. He was twenty-two. He'd worked at music stores and radio stations, and played accordion for dances. Then he decided to see the world outside Louisiana. He had a red Volvo station wagon. He drove all over the country for six months, pulled into Berkeley, liked the feel, and stayed. I've told you this, in slightly different words.

Boy Rob

Did he go to college with you?

Rob's Mother

No, honey. Your daddy was a musician. Some musicians don't learn at a school. They learn from other musicians. Daddy didn't have notebooks and pencils and books. He had records.

Aunt Jessica

Like about a ton of 'em in the back of that car. The rear bumper, I swear, was kissing the ground.

Aunt June

Good old Anne-Marie. I always knew when you guys were coming 'cause you could hear that car six blocks away. Kind of like the train.

Aunt Jessica

Kind of like the Concorde.

Rob

I used to think that was the reason. If you talk about your wish, it won't come true. And we talked.

Rob's Mother

Of course we talked. You needed some answers.

Rob

[reading]

"In second grade, Miss Rolf filled the blackboard with adjectives starting with *d*. We were supposed to write the word 'Daddy,' then pick five words from the board and write them list-style below: a Father's Day poem. I didn't know enough about my father to choose. Miss Rolf tried hard to talk me into 'dandy' as a start, a word I didn't like. To her annoyance, I finally wrote 'DJ' five times, a word not on the list. This was my first poem."

Rob

So how did you meet? The real story, now that I'm not five anymore.

Rob's Mother

He'd hooked up with a fiddler and was playing in a little club on Telegraph that had a dance floor. Some friends and I went. Cajun dancing was just catching on. They played a string of fast songs and then let the dancers catch their breath with a waltz. The waltz was "Little Black Eyes." And I fell in love—with the song and with him. When that happens, you find an excuse to make contact. In old movies, you see women drop their handkerchiefs.

Rob

And you guys?

Rob's Mother

He borrowed my jumper cables. Two weeks after that, he moved in. My parents were less than thrilled. I can still hear Grandpa—

Rob's Grandfather

What's that opening line in *Pride and Prejudice*, about a man who's got money—

Rob's Mother

"It is a truth universally acknowledged, that a single man . . ."

Rob's Grandmother

". . . in possession of a good fortune, must be in want of a wife."

Rob's Grandfather

Very good. Except he doesn't possess a fortune. He's not even making minimum wage. And he's moving into your apartment, Rose, instead of you moving to his manor in Sussex.

Rob's Grandmother
Yes, dear. That's often the way it's done these days. It comes of reading Tom Robbins instead of Jane Austen. You must speak to the English department about it.

Rob
What was he like?

Rob's Mother
Well, he lived up to the Cajun brochure. Dark-haired and handsome. Mustache. Muscular. Rough-hewn charm. Loved eating. He knew where every milligram of meat was hiding in a crab. He was a night owl—a gene he slipped to you. A good cook, but not much on doing the dishes after. He had a big smile and mischievous eyes. Sociable on the surface but really he was solitary at heart. He burrowed into his music and was gone. It was like he was communing with the old guys on his records. But what really hooked me about him was his ear.

Rob
His ear?

Rob's Mother
He'd listen to an airplane, find the tone in the scale, hum it, then invent some little tune and let the airplane be the drone. Refrigerators, motor scooters,

fans, anything. He was like a dog—he heard sounds most people couldn't. And he remembered them. You could pull out any album in his collection, play just two seconds of some scratchy field recording of some long-dead-and-buried Cajun fiddler who sounded like every other Cajun fiddler, and he'd tell you exactly who was playing. He couldn't read a note of music on a page, but he could hear a new song once and play it right back to you. He remembered where he was the first time he'd heard every song he knew—and who he was with and what they were drinking. I was studying languages and I was impressed. My ear's good, but I'm better at reading and writing. I learned French by *reading* French grammar books and novels, with some travel thrown in. I'm really an eye person. Lenny was pure ear.

Teacher
[reading]

"Richard receives twenty dollars for his birthday. He spends five dollars on video games and three dollars on candy. Laura also receives twenty dollars for her birthday. She spends two dollars on stationery for thank-you notes. What percentage—"

Boy Rob

Why?

Teacher

Why what?

Boy Rob

Why is Laura always so much better than Richard? Or does he buy stationery later maybe?

Teacher

I'm afraid I really can't answer that, Rob. They're not real people. Let's keep going, class.

Rob

[reading]

"Like Richard and Laura in math problems, like the Valdez family in our Spanish book, like the faces on billboards, my father was a character, a fiction, not flesh. He might have been Richard and Laura's father. When I felt discouraged about finding him, I used to picture him spending the holidays at the Valdez house, opening presents with Carlos and Marisol. Or I imagined him laughing with the smiling beer drinker in the billboard on Sixteenth, just out of sight to the left. That unreal realm was his home. When we drove to Colorado one summer, I checked every billboard, half expecting to glimpse him."

Rob

So what happened?

Rob's Mother

Well, he moved in. And he stayed. I'd never had a live-in boyfriend before. I felt I was finally an adult, like my official card had come in the mail. We were a couple. Rose and Lenny. Lenny and Rose. Invitations came in both of our names. People wrote us in their address books together. It's so confirming to be part of a couple. We moved to a tiny house on Panoramic, in the Berkeley hills. A woodstove in the living room for heat, a bathroom sink you could barely fit both hands in. He'd play accordion out on this redwood stump while I cooked or studied. I couldn't see him out there, but I loved hearing him, hearing his presence. I got my credential and my first job, part time. Lenny was playing weekends and had DJ jobs. We were happy. We were in love. I smiled for two years. And then I got pregnant.

Rob
So I was an accident.

Rob's Mother
No you weren't. Not in my mind. Never. Two years seemed plenty of time to know if we were compatible, which we were. We loved each other. I didn't see why it should ever end. Neither of us was looking elsewhere. So it felt natural to move on to the next stage. Or it did to me. Lenny saw it a little differently.

Lenny
'Cause music works as good as food. Brings back the old times and the old folks. Makes your wallpaper change right there on the wall—

Boy Rob
"—to what you had when you were a baby, or maybe to when you and your baby first met."

Rob's Mother
[singing a lullaby]
"Cuckoo, cuckoo,
What do you do?
In April I open my bill,
In May I sing night and day—"

Rob
So what did he do, when you told him?

Rob's Mother
He assumed I'd get an abortion. Which would have been easy to do. When I said I didn't want to, we had a big blowup. And to think I thought he'd be so happy. Instead, he slept at a friend's for a week. We talked some more. I thought he'd come around, but he didn't. He turned up the drinking a couple of notches. I was so torn. I didn't want to lose him, but I didn't want to lose you either. I felt ready for a child. I knew I'd make a good mother. My first teaching job was a horror, so staying home with a baby sounded like paradise. Back and forth, the arguing went on—until it was too late to get an abortion. Somewhere there, I'd crossed a line, like crossing the equator on a ship—

invisible, but real. And when I'd crossed it, I knew I was going to be a mother. The arguments changed, from "If we have a baby" to "When the baby comes." Lenny noticed the difference. And he knew he wasn't ready. Which he wasn't. He knew himself. I was the one who'd misjudged. I told him I was going ahead no matter what he did, that the decision and the responsibility were mine, which they were. I thought this might take the pressure off and that maybe then he'd accept the idea. Two days after that, I came home from work—I was in my fifth month—and all his things were gone.

Rob
Jesus. It was me. I caused the breakup.

Rob's Mother
You did no such thing. Hey, remember? We've talked about this. You're not responsible for someone else's reactions. Lenny might have been the type to be thrilled. He wasn't—but that's not your fault.

Aunt Jessica
You? You were positively edible, the cutest little boy on the planet. When I saw you, suddenly I was ready for kids. But Nick was still pretty undecided. And since you didn't have a dad, I'd push him to take you to baseball games and things—remember? Hoping, you know, he'd get into being a father. Sort of a trial offer.

                    Rob
Yeah, I remember.

                  Boy Rob
I have to go to the bathroom.

                    Nick
What?

                  Boy Rob
I need to go to the bathroom.

                    Nick
Now?

                  Boy Rob
Yeah.

                    Nick
Are you kidding? The bases are loaded! You
don't—you don't want to miss what happens, do you?

                  Boy Rob
I need to pee. Really bad.

                    Nick
Christ, I don't believe it. *We're not missing this.*

                  Boy Rob
But I need to go.

Nick

Fine! Pee in this.

Boy Rob

But there's still popcorn in it.

Rob

What did you do, after he left?

Rob's Mother

I called in sick and cried. For two days. The next morning, I cleaned house from top to bottom. I sewed curtains for the window, spackled cracks, repainted. And I went out and bought a cradle I couldn't afford. Teachers at work gave me sacks of clothes. And suddenly, without the shouting matches, I was looking forward to the birth. I tried to focus on that instead of the fear about going it alone. I'd lost Lenny, but I was about to get you. And I knew you'd never leave. Right?

Rob

Right. I'll still be here sharing the bathroom with you when I'm eighty and you're a hundred and five, or whatever. Was it hard, you know, giving birth without a husband there like everyone else?

Rob's Mother

I was envious of the couples. But it's not like I was squatting in a ditch somewhere. I had a fabulous midwife. Eleven hours of labor. Which is nothing, but enough to get the idea, believe me. I felt like I'd run three marathons and swum out to Alcatraz and back. When you finally came out and they put you on my chest, I barely had the strength to hold you. I rested a minute. Then I looked at you. And there was his nose and his lips. You opened your eyes—so dark and shiny. And I heard "Little Black Eyes" in my head. And I started crying.

Rob

Did he come to the hospital?

Rob's Mother

No, but he wouldn't have known which one I was in. He did call up June a few weeks later, to see if you'd been born. He asked about your name and your birthday and how you were doing. He never visited, never called. He was still working at an oldies station—I used to listen just to check. Once in a while I'd see Anne-Marie parked somewhere, but I didn't know where he was living. Then, maybe six months later, I walked in the door, and he'd been there. Lying in the cradle was the sound-effects record. On top of it was the tape of the oldies show. As soon as I saw, I had a feeling he was gone. Which he was. I called the station and they told me he'd quit and was moving. No forwarding address.

Rob's Grandfather

I never liked accordions anyway. Or accordion players.

Boy Rob

How come everyone hates accordions?

Rob's Grandfather

It's called good taste.

Rob's Grandmother

It's called guilt by association. *If* you like the accordion, *then* you must like Lawrence Welk. The Red-baiters used this tactic all the time in the fifties.

Rob's Grandfather

So why didn't they get Lawrence Welk off the air and into prison where he belonged?

Rob's Grandmother

The accordion is a fine instrument, Robbie.

Rob's Grandfather

Some forms of expression the First Amendment doesn't cover. Obscenity, inciting to riot, and accordion playing. The Founding Fathers *loathed* the accordion.

Rob's Grandmother

It hadn't even been invented. Your grandpa's making up history again.

Rob's Grandfather
John Adams wanted the *death penalty*—

Rob's Grandmother
Don't listen to Grandpa.

Rob's Mother
[singing]
"In April I open my bill,
In May I sing night and day,
In June I change my tune—"

Aunt June
Those birds there? Sure they'll migrate. They're all done raising their babies. They'll be flying down to Mexico any week now.

Boy Rob
But then they fly back. I mean later. Right?

Rob's Mother
I don't know where he found that album. *Sounds of a Southern Swamp.* He liked it here, but he missed Louisiana. He missed cane syrup and crawfish in the spring and fireflies and even humidity. When the fog would come in in July and it was freezing, he couldn't believe it. I'd find that record on the turntable. He liked to play it late at night. It meant a lot to him. I'm surprised he gave it up. He was possessive with his records. But he wanted you to know where he was

from, and where you're from, too. Same with the tape of his show. It was his way of telling you who he was. A picture tells a thousand words. But you get a thousand pictures from somebody's voice.

Rob's Grandmother
[reading]

"Legacy. 1. A gift of property, especially personal property, by will; a bequest. 2. Anything handed down from the past, as from an ancestor or predecessor."

Rob
[reading]

"I fantasized his return constantly. I watched for red Volvo station wagons. I knew what he looked like from photographs and I looked for him in crowds, in passing cars, in the background of newspaper photos, at Giants games. I saw him in books, as well. He was the missing person in my grandmother's mysteries. I was the detective on his trail."

Opera Radio Host

As Act Two opens, three years have passed since Pinkerton's departure. Madame Butterfly, however, has not given up hope, and in response to her servant's pessimism she sings her famous aria, *Un bel dì*, describing in detail how he will one day sail into the harbor, come up the hill, and once again—

Rob's Mother, Grandparents, Aunts
[singing]
Happy Birthday, dear Robbie—

Aunt Jessica
You got all the candles!

Rob's Grandfather
He always does.

Rob
[reading]
"I believed that I could bring him back. I would reform. If I got myself up every morning without my mother having to wake me, he'd come back. If I got straight A's in school, he'd come back. If I saved all my birthday and Christmas money and didn't spend any on me, he'd come back. I saw signs and omens. I studied the outcomes of 49er-Saints football games for hidden meanings. I never missed the weather report for New Orleans. That one line in the newspaper—the high, low, and precipitation figure—was like a keyhole through which I could almost see him. When the new phone book came out every year, I checked for 'Guidry' and called up any new candidates I hadn't tried before, hoping he was still nearby."

Woman on Telephone
Sorry, darlin'. There's no Leonard here. I don't give out my name, but it sure ain't Leonard.

Boy Rob

Do you *know* a Leonard Guidry? Is he maybe in your family?

Woman on Telephone

In my family? Hmmm. Well, let's see. We got us a Leroy. You want him? Honey, you can have him, 'cause he's a mean son of a—

Rob
[reading]

"My campaign was private, invisible to others, never revealed even to my mother. Ineffective charms were replaced by new ones. Every brown pelican I saw—Louisiana's state bird—brought his return a day closer. Days I didn't hear an accordion pushed his return a day back. I began to think of the long stairway in our house as the Mississippi. The landing was St. Louis and the bottom step was Louisiana. I stepped on it twice, to show I hadn't forgotten him."

Aunt June

Most migrating birds breed in the north, then go south for the winter. But brown pelicans are different. The ones we have here breed down in Mexico and the Channel Islands, then they fly *north*. Exactly the opposite of what most birds do.

Boy Rob

Are you sure?

Rob

I remember when you said that, it seemed a bad sign. I wanted a father who was like all the others.

Aunt June

Of course you did.

Rob's Mother
[singing]
"In May I sing night and day,
In June I change my tune,
In July far, far I fly
In August—"

Rob
[reading]
"In fifth grade, we studied the myth of Theseus, each student reading a paragraph from the book aloud. Theseus doesn't know who his father is, but knows the secret is buried under a huge stone. When he's sixteen, he's strong enough to move the stone, and finds underneath it a pair of sandals and a sword with the royal insignia of Athens. His father is king of Athens, and left these tokens to identify himself. I felt myself flushing, felt sure all eyes were on me. I was so astounded, I couldn't find my voice to read. My father, too, had left me tokens."

Lenny
By request, the Beatles doing "Yesterday" for—

Boy Rob

—another satisfied customer here on "The Ghost Raising." Lenny here till one A.M.

Rob

You know what I admire? That you never made me hate him. When Zad's parents got divorced, her mother took an X-acto knife and cut her father out of all the photos. But you put a framed photo right there on my dresser.

Lenny

It's not always that easy, tracking down requests. Sometimes I spend a whole afternoon checking the used record shops—

Rob's Grandfather

I swear to God, if I hear that tape one more time—

Rob's Grandmother

Shhh! He'll hear you!

Rob's Mother

You were a night person. Future Bartenders of America, Infant Auxiliary. But I was a morning person. I need nine hours a night. I was getting maybe five, then dropping you off at day care and going to teach. I could hardly speak English, much less Spanish or French. The landlord raised the rent, then he hit the roof when he found out there was a baby in the house.

He doubled the deposit. Without Lenny's pay, I had to go to full time, but day care was eating up half my pay. Gas was eating up the rest—I was commuting all the way to Menlo Park. In winter, it was dark by the time I picked you up. I felt I was missing your childhood. The apartment here was empty. I wasn't proud. Yes, I was moving back in with my parents. But the rent they were charging was so low I could go back to part time and to being your mother. Grandma had just retired, so no more day care. No more commuting across the bay. And Grandma's a night owl, like you. To let me catch up on my sleep, she'd keep you overnight there a couple times a week, playing and reading to you. You were the first grandchild. They were in heaven.

Rob's Grandfather
He knocked over his juice, that's what. I told you—not in a tall glass. *And not cranberry.*

Rob's Grandmother
It was probably time to get the carpet cleaned anyway.

Rob's Grandfather
Well it wasn't time to get this shirt cleaned! I've got a class in an hour and I look like I've been attacked with a machete. I really don't have time—

Rob's Grandmother
Go on! Go! I'll finish up! Just like thirty years ago!

Rob
[reading]

"Theseus immediately set off for Athens. But no one knew where my father was. So I went searching. I did this at night. I did it on the radio."

2nd Radio Announcer
KNBR, San Francisco, 680.

3rd Radio Announcer
Charlie Grant with you till midnight—

Radio Psychic
I'm sensing something quite vulnerable in your aura, Shana. I'm wondering if maybe you've suffered a setback, maybe something seemingly minor, perhaps a loss of some sort, something fairly recent, or perhaps in the past?

Psychic Show Caller
How could you know that? You're so amazing.

Rob
[reading]

"I wasn't taller than my mother until ninth grade, but I could stay awake later from a much earlier age. In grammar school, when she was asleep, I'd stay up. I'd have my headphones on. Sometimes I'd turn off all the lights in my room and look out at the lights on the Bay Bridge. I'd make sure my door was closed. And then I'd go hunting for my father. He could be anywhere on the dial. He was Lenny Guidry, but he might be 'Leonard Goodrich' at a classical station, as my mother had said he'd once been. I figured he'd be 'Leo' or 'Len' or 'Lenny' playing top forty or oldies. 'LG' playing jazz. 'Leonardo' doing psychic readings. Or maybe just a nameless voice reading the news or doing the Civil Defense System test. I feared he might work at an FM station; their signals are line-of-sight and don't carry far. Or worse—what if he weren't actually on the air, but was flying the traffic helicopter, or filing CDs, or working the wah-wah pedal at the Spanish stations."

Spanish DJ
Ochocientos ochenta, la voz de San José-é-é-é-é!

4th Radio Announcer
—what it really means to live in Christ, to go to Him and ask Him to take your—

5th Radio Announcer
Jeff in Oakland, your thoughts on the Raiders' kicking game.

Rob
[reading]
"It was incredible. I was alone in my bedroom, but with the radio, it was as if there were a huge party in the house and I was going room to room, eavesdropping. There was a rock band playing in the living room,

mariachi music in the backyard, a vet diagnosing symptoms in the hall, pranksters calling up listeners on our telephone in the kitchen. I liked hearing DJs start their shifts—the partylike banter, joking with the engineer. Station sign-offs, by contrast, felt grim: a solemn voice reading a statement, lists of translator stations, sometimes a bit of ceremonial music, and then—nothing."

1st Radio Announcer
In compliance with the Federal Communications Commission—

2nd Radio Announcer
—will resume transmission at—

3rd Radio Announcer
K217CR, ninety-two point four, Morgan Hill. K256AE eighty-nine point—

4th Radio Announcer
This concludes our—

5th Radio Announcer
—is now going off the air.

[pause]

Rob
[reading]
"Listening to the static where the signal had been

was like witnessing a death. Sign-offs seemed to tell me my father was nowhere to be found. I tried not to hear them."

Rob's Mother

I still had a book of nursery rhymes from when I was a child. Sometimes I'd sing them to you, and I'd realize I was singing the same tune I'd heard Grandma use when she'd sung them to me.

Rob
[reading]

"Instead of radio, sometimes I'd listen to the sound-effects record late at night. I made a tape of it so I could play it in my room. I closed my eyes and imagined myself in a little cabin on the edge of a swamp. My father was on the porch with me. We were both in rocking chairs, rocking slowly. I didn't know what it would be like to talk to him, so I imagined that we weren't talking, just listening to the sounds."

Rob's Mother
[singing]

"In May I sing night and day,
In June I change my tune,
In July far, far I fly,
In August away I must."

Rob
[reading]

"That was the one I remember the most. You'd

have thought my mother would have avoided it. Later I realized it was her way of telling me that he was destined to go, not to get my hopes up, that there was nothing anyone could do about it. A few years after that, I realized something else—that she'd been telling the very same thing to herself."

[We hear the sound-effects recording. It begins fading out after half a minute, overlapping the following speech.]

1st Male Caller
—can't remember who did it, one of those groups from the fifties, what were they called? The New Tones? The Two Tones? [Hums a tune hopelessly off-key.] *You've heard it a million times. It was a big, big hit.* [Hums some more.] *Know the one I mean?*

Lenny
I'm afraid I don't. I tried. I really did. Sent your message to a lab for spectroscopic musical analysis and tune matching from their bank of two million melodies, and the closest match they came up with was this shaman's chant to cure leprosy from the Solomon Islands. And unfortunately, we don't have that in the studio. Let's see who else called.

2nd Male Caller
Hi, Lenny. Hey, it's our twenty-fifth wedding anniversary, so I said we should request something, and she said, how about "Ninety-eight Tears." So I said it's "Ninety-six Tears," by Question Mark and the Mysterians, you know,

from the sixties, but she says it's ninety-eight, so we had a little discussion about it, but she's stubborn, so I said I'd call in. She'll believe you but not me, is what it boils down to. We don't actually want to hear it—I can't stand that song. All I want is for you to tell her, right here, on the air—

Mr. McCarthy

"Music, when soft voices die, vibrates in the memory." Percy Bysshe Shelley. A famous line. You autobiographers are in search of that music and those vibrations. Has anyone here been up in the bell tower at Berkeley just at the moment when the bells stop?

Rob's Grandmother
[reading]

"You owe me ten shillings,
Say the bells of St. Helen's.
When will you pay me?
Say the bells of Old Bailey.
When I grow rich,
Say the bells of Shoreditch."

1st Radio Announcer

Traffic of course very light at this hour. A stall on the Bay Bridge, upper deck. The accident on Eight-Eighty. That's about it. Back to you, Kyle and Maria.

2nd Radio Announcer

—from his 1961 release on the Decca label. I'm Alex, playing all the jazz that's fit to play.

3rd Radio Announcer
Are you tired of itching, burning feet? Coming up, Dr. Karl Engelmann will tell you about an amazing—

4th Radio Announcer
Jenny Smith, taking your calls about relationships, family, the holidays—

5th Radio Announcer
And don't forget to stay tuned for the postgame show with Rick and Ron.

1st Radio Announcer
Mike Russo with this news update—

2nd Radio Announcer
Carrie, playing all your country favorites—

3rd Radio Announcer
El Lobo with you till five A.M.—

4th Radio Announcer
The Reverend Bob Cuthbert—

5th Radio Announcer
Chuckie G.—

Rob's Grandmother
[reading]
"When I grow rich,

Say the bells of Shoreditch.
When will that be?
Say the bells at Stepney.
I'm sure I don't know,
Says the great bell at Bow."

Rob
[reading]

"Radio was an ocean of names. When would I hear his? I didn't know, but that didn't stop me from searching."

1st Radio Announcer

—Christy, Jim, Brett, and the whole KCBS news team.

Rob
[reading]

"By sixth grade, I'd begun to lose hope in the local stations. If he missed Louisiana so much, he'd probably returned, or at least gone someplace with heat and swamps and fireflies. That year, I began concentrating on the out-of-state stations. In the radio world, 'DX' means distance. I became an AM band DXer."

Ray

It's like this, chief. When the sun goes down, the radio waves go higher in the atmosphere without getting absorbed. You learned about the ionosphere in school, right? They shoot up through the D level and get all the way to the F, maybe a hundred and fifty miles up. And then *Bam*! They bounce off the F at an angle and come back, maybe a hundred, maybe a thousand, maybe a couple thousand miles from where they started. That's called skip. And skip, my friend, is your friend.

2nd Radio Announcer
JT, sitting in for EJ, chillin' with y'all till—

3rd Radio Announcer
Wally Clark—

4th Radio Announcer
—and Paula Dinsmore—

3rd Radio Announcer
—here with you for the radio swap meet. If you've got something to sell or trade—

4th Radio Announcer
—preferably not recently stolen—

Rob
[reading]
"I saved my money and replaced my portable with a stereo tuner. I started looking in the window, then standing in the door, then meandering the aisles like a shoplifter at Ray's Electronics on Sixteenth. It was dim as a cave and crammed with old equipment. Ray kept

two ashtrays busy at a time, one at the phone and one on the counter, enveloping the shop in its own atmosphere composed of two percent oxygen and ninety-eight percent cigarette smoke, the price of his otherwise free advice."

Ray
Twilight's when you can pick up the little guys. At night the big guns come out—fifty thousand kilowatts and more. Instead of out, they're aiming a lot of their signal up and counting on skip to really increase their range.

5th Radio Announcer
Jimmy Gadsen with the Gospel Express—

1st Radio Announcer
—and calling all the play-by-play, here's Frank Balasteri.

Rob's Grandfather
What do you mean, no fluorescent lights?

Boy Rob
Ray says that's what's causing the buzzing on the radio.

Rob's Grandmother
You need a new desk light anyway.

Rob's Grandfather
No, I don't!

Rob's Grandmother
Or you could wait till Robbie's asleep to use it.

Rob's Grandfather
What am I—Anne Frank in my own house? Next it'll be no loud foods. No raw carrots!

2nd Radio Announcer
—at Fairhaven Mall from noon to four with yours truly, Doyle Lindeborg, along with many of your other favorite radio personalities—

Rob
[reading]
"While everyone else listened to the local stations, I loitered in the gaps in between, hoping for distant signals. This requires patience, a sharp ear, and a steady hand. I could turn a knob slower than any boy in California. I ventured east into the Central Valley: Mexican music, tubas pumping like steam engines, country western stations with weepy steel guitars, the farm report, ads for pesticides, preachers requesting donations to be sent to Redding or Fresno or Bakersfield. Sometimes, I'd pick up Eugene, Oregon, or KKOB in Albuquerque. It was thrilling to be able to search at such a distance. And yet, what if I found him,

happily settled so far from us, with no thought of ever coming back?"

3rd Radio Announcer
—so pleased you're with us tonight and that you're part of our radio family of the air.

Rob
[reading]
"No matter how distant, radio was much the same everywhere. And anyone could join the family of listeners. The out-of-state announcers were my great-uncles and second cousins, less familiar than the locals but still relatives."

4th Radio Announcer
KCWW, Tempe, Arizona, where the time is ten past midnight. Nat Winston spending the wee hours—

Rob
[reading]
"My aunt June had a telescope, and I loved to close my eyes, point it at no place in particular, and then peer through the eyepiece at that random circle of sky. One night I was doing the same with the radio, giving the tuning knob roulette-wheel spins, and I—"

5th Radio Announcer
That's right, Lenny. It'll be chilly this weekend—

Rob
[reading]

"My hair stood on end. The station was faint. I tuned it in better and turned the volume up all the way. I waited through the interminable weather report to hear Lenny's—"

1st Radio Announcer

Thank you, Doreen. Let's get back to the music, with Randy Travis doing—

Rob
[reading]

"He had a smooth, radio-school voice. I knew right away that it wasn't him. Still, it was the closest I'd gotten and I became a regular listener. The station was from Reno and played mainstream country. His last name was Gunderson. One night he mentioned 'the missus.' I waited for weeks to hear further details— children, interests, birthplace, anything—but all he did was announce strings of song titles. I gave up, but knew I'd scored a hit. There were Lennys out there. I just had to find the right one."

Ray

The sticker says twelve dollars. You got twelve dollars?

Boy Rob

No.

Ray

Then twelve dollars is just the "suggested retail price." A general guideline. How much you got to spend?

Boy Rob

Five dollars.

Ray

Sold.

Rob
[reading]

"I bought an old AM amp from Ray. He threw in some speaker wire for free and told me to tape it around my bedroom ceiling for an antenna. That night I pulled in Dallas, Texas. Then KTRH in Houston. I felt I was on my father's trail. Then—"

2nd Radio Announcer

High tomorrow, ninety-one degrees, relative humidity about the same, so stay cool out there. Drink plenty of liquids and keep your radio tuned to the coolest place on the dial—KWKH, Shreveport.

Rob
[reading]

"I'd found Louisiana. I could hardly believe it. It was foggy and frigid in San Francisco, but I could hear thunderstorms crackling along the line, scratching out the DJ's voice. They implied distance, dripping heat, little crossroad towns. The signal faded, fought back, faded again. I listened for hours. There was no mention of my father. Even so, I couldn't stop peering down on such a far-off, foreign place."

Rob's Grandmother
[reading]
"Camera obscura: A darkened boxlike device in which images of external and often distant objects, admitted through an aperture, are exhibited in their natural colors."

Boy Rob
[reading]
"Louisiana's major products are petroleum, natural gas, sugarcane, rice—"

3rd Radio Announcer
That's two touchdowns in the last three and a half minutes. The 49ers are just burying the Saints.

Rob's Mother
In Shreveport?

Boy Rob
Yeah.

Rob's Mother

Hmmm. I doubt it. His family's down around Lafayette, in the Cajun part of the state. Or they used to be. I tried calling once, but his parents must have moved. I guess they could be in Shreveport. It's up north. Pretty different worlds, from what he said.

Rob

[reading]

"I never heard another station in Louisiana. Still, I kept exploring at night, logging Kansas City, Minneapolis, Chicago. I've always had flying dreams—looking down on landscapes and towns far below. These are thrilling, but very rare. Radio gave me the same sensation on demand."

4th Radio Announcer

—pancake breakfast this coming Saturday, from eight to eleven, sponsored by the Fort Worth Elks Club. All you can eat, and let me tell you, you won't need to eat breakfast again for a week.

Aunt Jessica

I think it was for your twelfth birthday. I'd seen it in a catalog of educational toys at school. And I knew right away it was meant for you.

Aunt June

Jessica and I used to have a friendly competition

with the presents. I remember I gave you birding binoculars that year. I was sure she couldn't top that. But when you opened up that shortwave radio kit— she'd trumped me. *She* was your favorite aunt.

Rob
[reading]
    "Suddenly my radio flights increased vastly in distance."

Aunt Jessica
    Since it was a kit, I thought Nick could help you put it together. Another of my father-son, quality time get-togethers. Or that was the theory.

Nick
    You gotta be kidding. Listen to this! "Locate now wires H and J, vigilantly having remove insulations previous to solder to E and F respectfully, kindly to consult the Figure 12." Can you believe that? Every sentence is like that! This translator oughta go build his own electric chair *and then sit in it!*

Rob
Nick's not really all that mechanical, is he?

Aunt Jessica
He's a PE teacher. I thought that was enough.

Rob
[reading]

"My uncle knew nothing about electricity or radios. I was in middle school now and got advice from my sixth-grade science teacher. Nick and I wound wires around coils and soldered and glued and sneezed tiny washers off the table and cut ourselves and cursed for weeks. I later found out that it was at this time that he signed up for his vasectomy."

Rob's Mother

It was as if you were building Frankenstein. Working at night, smoke from the soldering iron, attaching a speaker instead of a voice box. And then when you finished and the moment finally came for plugging it in, sending electricity through it, and we all heard that high static, like a baby's first cry—

Aunt Jessica

And then the first station—

Rob's Mother

The creature's first words—

Aunt June

Wasn't it cricket scores?

Aunt Jessica

And even Nick smiled.

Rob's Grandmother
The sound of Big Ben tolling, very low, and then—

5th Radio Announcer
[British accent]
This is the World Service of the BBC.

Rob's Mother
It was like watching a boat being launched. Everyone clapped.

Rob
[reading]
"They celebrated. I waited for them to leave. The shortwave was more than a new toy. I remembered my mother's college friend who'd gotten a job broadcasting in English at Radio France. There was now nowhere on earth that I couldn't look for my father."

1st Radio Announcer
This is Sofia, Bulgaria, calling.

2nd Radio Announcer
You are tuned to Radio Australia, the overseas—

3rd Radio Announcer
—listening to the Voice of the Andes, broadcasting from Quito—

4th Radio Announcer
This is All India Radio—

5th Radio Announcer
You're tuned to the English service of the Far East Broadcasting Company, transmitting from the Philippines on fifteen-four-four-five, seventeen—

Rob
[reading]
"What speed is to race-car drivers, distance is to shortwave listeners. I was in love with distance. The shortwave had an AM band on which reception was far better than on my other radio, but the pull of the shortwave bands was much stronger. Along with stations broadcasting in every language, there was Morse Code and all sorts of unintelligible signals: pulsing, croaking, some bubbly as an aquarium pump, some like an endless threatening chord. Like moths thronging a porch light, they implied an unknown realm writhing with life."

1st Radio Announcer
It's nineteen hundred hours, time for "German by Radio" with your host—

2nd Radio Announcer
Radio New Zealand International's "Kiwi Music Hour," a regular—

3rd Radio Announcer
And now, a summary of news stories from Taiwan.

4th Radio Announcer

—as we open the mailbag here at Radio Nederland.

Rob
[reading]

"I began writing to stations, sending reception reports in exchange for QSL cards—verifications sent by stations, collected by shortwave listeners. A month later the mail began arriving. Along with the QSL might be a decal, a station schedule, a flag, a magazine, a banner, a map, or all of the above. I began getting more mail than my mother got. Some of it kept coming for years. I always checked the station manager's signature on the QSL, waiting to see the name 'Leonard Guidry.'"

Rob's Grandmother

What is it, Robbie?

Boy Rob

Another Christmas card. From Radio Norway. Look.

Rob's Grandfather

My own *brother* hasn't sent me a card in twenty years—and you get one from Radio Norway!

Rob
[reading]

"I met new kids in middle school. I made new

friends. We did homework together, played Ping-Pong in garages, hung out at malls. But my radio world was private. It became more public, however, the day I saw a baby monitor at a garage sale. I stood and stared at it for five minutes, not knowing why. Then, in a flash, I saw what it could do. I bought it for a dollar, plugged the speaker in near my mother's bed, and took the microphone into my room."

Rob's Mother
Remember? Of course I remember. I wrote a poem about it, called "Sign On."

Boy Rob
It's seven-thirteen on this sunny Saturday morning in San Francisco, except that in the time it took to say that it's now actually seven-thirteen and fifteen seconds, seven-thirteen and twenty seconds, twenty-five seconds, thirty seconds, anyway, you're tuned to K-Rob, so don't touch that dial, which you can't anyway 'cause it's set to just this one frequency—

Rob's Mother
The programming content was a little thin, but the concept was fabulous. I was dead asleep. I had no idea where it was coming from.

Rob
It was right there in the bookcase over your bed, but I hid it with a T-shirt. I set my alarm to wake up before you.

Boy Rob

If you have any requests, for oldies or newies or anything else, don't pick up the phone, just yell down the hall, and I'll do my best to track 'em down. I may have to call up my team of experts and wake them up, too, but that's OK, *because they're really sleeping way too late when they ought to be listening to the radio!*

Rob's Mother

My head cleared and I figured it out. And I lay there and listened, smiling and laughing. The first of so many mornings.

Boy Rob

Over to you, Rob, in Traffic-copter Two. How's it look?

Rob's Grandmother

And then, remember? He'd use the electric pencil sharpener, to sound like the helicopter engine.

Rob's Mother

Till every pencil in the house was half an inch long.

Boy Rob

"There's no traffic coming in on the Golden Gate, Ed. Not a single car. Same with the Richmond and the Bay Bridge." "What is this, Rob, some kind of joke? It's Monday." "It's not *my* fault, Ed. There's *just no cars!* None driving, parked, anywhere." "My God, I'm looking out the window, and you're right. This is too weird!

Something's very, very wrong. Mabel—start the Civil
Defense siren!"

Rob's Mother
And you'd gotten a real siren somewhere.

Rob
In a junk shop.

Rob's Mother
Good old Mabel and Ed. I miss K-Rob. What was
next?

Rob
There was KOP. I had a couple of different ones
running at the same time. And I was still listening to
shortwave.

Boy Rob
[reading]
"It was a rotten business, detective work, and at
the moment business was rotten. He'd quit the racket
once and sworn he'd never come back. But here he
was—his name on the door and his feet on the desk."

Rob's Grandmother
You were a very good reader. "KOP—your station
for cops and robbers." And then the siren. Which was
really quite loud, I have to admit. And that first time,
when you took us by surprise—

Rob
And Grandpa thought it was an earthquake, the Big One—

Rob's Mother
And then the heart palpitations and the emergency room.

Rob's Grandmother
He was fine. And Robbie didn't mean to scare him.

5th Radio Announcer
—a program of Czech music and interviews here on Radio Prague International.

1st Radio Announcer
At the tone, the time will be twenty-three hundred hours, Coordinated Universal Time.

2nd Radio Announcer
—up-to-the-minute sports scores on the Armed Forces Radio Network, beamed to Europe at—

Aunt June
Sure. You slept over at my place. And in the morning, out of nowhere I heard this duck screeching in my ear.

Boy Rob
"Ninety-one point five, KWAK, quack radio, all

birds, all the time. And here's Rob, with the morning bird report." "Thanks, Joe. We've got heavy pelican traffic northbound, from Half Moon Bay all the way—"

Aunt June

You were like a kid with one of those buzzer rings—you had to spring it on everybody. You'd packed the baby monitor in your bag. Along with that bird call I'd given you.

Rob
[reading]

"Had my father made up his own stations, too? What had I inherited from him? I liked Cajun music, but was hopeless at playing musical instruments. I would take the few pictures of him we had, go into the bathroom, lock the door, and compare our noses in the mirror, then our eyes, chins, left profiles, right profiles. I wondered what he looked like now. I wondered if I would look like him."

Rob's Mother

Then there was the station for Mr. and Mrs. Kathos. You put the speaker on the kitchen windowsill.

Boy Rob

You're tuned to KERG—that's "Greek" backwards. The high in Athens today will be sixty-one, partly cloudy—

Rob

I got the weather from the *Chronicle*, and you had a tape of Greek music. A custom-made radio station—and both of them were too hard of hearing to notice. The speaker was just so crummy. It was horrible.

Ray

What do you expect? It's a baby monitor. You got it for a buck, my friend. With a buck you get popcorn, not Chicken Kiev.

Rob
[reading]

"So Ray sold me a public address amp, a mike, and a twenty-watt speaker. My stations were no longer mobile, but the sound was infinitely better."

Boy Rob
[cultured accent]

And now Sophia Pizzeria, who sang the part of Carmen, enters from the left to a very enthusiastic ovation.

Aunt Jessica

I bought you that CD with all the sound effects, remember? Screams, church bells, squealing tires—

Boy Rob

She bows, receives a bouquet of roses from a stagehand, and warmly acknowledges the conductor and orchestra. She blows kisses to the left. Now to the right. And now she takes a very deep bow—

[sound of bones cracking]

—and, good Lord, she can't seem to straighten up. Apparently she bowed *too* deeply. The stagehand returns now and tries to straighten her, to very warm applause.

[sound of bones cracking]

No luck there. Dear me.

Aunt Jessica
You really got a lot of use out of the bone-cracking track.

Boy Rob
It's time now, listeners, for radio aerobics. Let's begin with a few easy warmups. Bring your left arm around behind your back as far as you can.

[sound of bones cracking]

Good. Now stretch those legs wide apart.

[sound of bones cracking]

Rob's Grandmother
What I liked best were the stories you'd do completely out of sounds. They were like dreams. You must have had a turntable and a tape player and a CD player.

You'd have the swamp sounds going for a while all alone, then on top of that you'd put accordion music, real soft—

Rob
[reading]
"I'd imagine us in our cabin, at night, rocking in the dark, unable to see each other, him playing his accordion—"

Rob's Grandmother
Then suddenly there might be a scream. Or footsteps. Then maybe bells—

Audiobook Reader
"Hear the sledges with the bells—
Silver bells!"

Rob
[reading]
"Could it be, I wondered, that DJ behavior was carried in a gene? If so, my actions weren't my own. I had no control over what I was doing or who I was becoming. And yet, this meant he was with me, inside me. He was willing me to copy him. It was he who was willing me to search for him—which proved that he wanted to be found."

Rob's Grandmother
The footsteps would keep going, but now we'd be

in London. You'd taped Big Ben off your shortwave.
We'd hear it tolling, over and over.

Rob
[reading]
"I began falling asleep at the shortwave. I was getting
closer. I would never give up. He wouldn't let me."

Rob's Grandmother
Then maybe one of Churchill's speeches from the
war. Or you'd play something from a book on tape. You
were big on Poe back then and you had this wonderful
tape of his stories and poems. "Annabel Lee," and the
one about the bells—

Audiobook Reader
"To the tintinnabulation that so musically wells
From the bells, bells, bells—"

Aunt June
Sure, a few of them. Maybe it's cloudy and they
can't see the stars—which is probably how they navigate.
Or storms can blow birds way off course. They're
called vagrants. They might end up on the wrong side
of the continent, or on the wrong continent altogeth-
er. Then, next season, they get back on track.

Audiobook Reader
"Hear the mellow wedding bells
Golden bells!

What a world of happiness their harmony foretells!
Through the balmy air of night—"

Rob
[reading]

"Toward the end of eighth grade, instead of losing hope, I felt surer than ever that the meeting with my father was approaching. I was about to turn thirteen, a year behind my classmates, the result of skipping second grade. I saw that my birthday would fall on the last day of school in June. This striking conjunction had never happened before. I knew from my mother that birthdays were important to him. He'd thrown her a surprise party one year. More important, his own family had given him a huge party for his thirteenth, at which he'd received his first accordion. I knew that my father was aware of my birth date. And I knew that thoughts, like radio waves, skip thousands of miles. He might not have heard my living-room stations, but I knew he was thinking about me. And I knew he'd want to be a part of my gates-of-adulthood birthday. I'd caught my mother talking very softly on the phone lately. He'd no doubt find out about graduation and would want to be there for that momentous event as well."

Audiobook Reader

"How it swells!
How it dwells
On the Future! how it tells—"

Ray

Now for FM stations, there's E skip. That's when the big solar flares come and the E layer up in the atmosphere gets ionized real strong in places. You can pick up stations you'd never have a chance for.

Boy Rob

When does that happen?

Ray

Coming up in June, my friend. Mark your calendar.

Rob
[reading]
"June. Everything was lining up. And then the bottom stair suddenly began squeaking. The Louisiana stair."

Audiobook Reader
"Of the rapture that impels—"

Rob
[reading]
"He was a vagrant bird who'd gotten off track. But now he was coming back. I could feel it, the way a tree feels it's spring. When I woke on that long-awaited day, my heart was beating as it never had on a Christmas morning. It was a belfry. My whole body was ringing."

Audiobook Reader
"To the swinging and the ringing
Of the bells, bells, bells—"

Rob's Mother
We'd decided to celebrate your birthday after the graduation ceremony, which started at six—

Aunt Jessica
—and lasted about fourteen hours. The speeches, the orchestra, the chorus—

Rob's Grandfather
—the board of education stumping for reelection. And my God, the kids marching so slowly down the aisles like they had leg chains on, thousands of kids. My *entire college* didn't have that many kids.

Rob
[reading]
"It didn't seem long or slow to me. My feet only appeared to be on the ground. I was floating, as in one of my dreams. When I walked down the aisle, looking straight ahead as they'd taught us, I could feel his eyes on my back, and I smiled. I wondered about what to say, then decided I'd let him do the talking at the start. A second skin of sweat covered me. My fingertips tingled. When I finally reached the stage and turned, I spotted my family near the front. The auditorium was deep and packed, a confetti of faces, those in the rear third

shadowed by the balcony. Looking at me, no one knew that I was busy adding thirteen years to his photo, searching out candidates, ranking them, trying to make out the faces in the back."

Rob's Mother
I kept looking at you, but your eyes were aimed over my head. You were so lost in yourself that you didn't hear your name—

Rob
—called for the scholarship award. Thank you. I do remember that, with everyone's help over the years— like every single time I forget anything.

Rob's Grandfather
What I remember is that everyone's butts went numb sitting in those wooden seats and the next year they put in brand-new upholstered ones.

Rob's Grandmother
Thanks, no doubt, to your timely letter.

Rob
[reading]
"We got our diplomas one by one. Amazingly, they spelled 'Radkovitz' correctly. Miracles were in the air. Alphabetically, row by row, we filed back down and outside to the courtyard. By the time I arrived, it was mobbed. I squeezed onto a bench and stood—not to

find my family, but so my father could find me. I waved my arms discreetly, at no one in particular. I thought to myself—"

Boy Rob
You're crazy. He's not here. Don't wave your arms. How did you talk yourself into this?

Rob
[reading]
"Then in my mind other voices answered back—"

Ray
Radio men sorta have a sixth sense, between themselves. I had three other radio buddies in Korea—

3rd Radio Announcer
—part of our radio family of the air.

4th Radio Announcer
—as he reminds us in Second Corinthians, "For we walk by faith, not by sight."

Rob
[reading]
"My family found me and took pictures. My eyes were everywhere but on the camera. Then I felt a hand on my shoulder. I whirled around. I looked into the face. It was my English teacher. I felt him search out my hand, felt him shake it. I remember nothing of what he said. I made the excuse of looking for friends

and circulated through the crowd, waiting to be noticed: a lost dog in a strange part of town. Nobody claimed me. The crowd eventually began melting away. I told myself that I hadn't really thought he'd come, though I knew this was false. Then I countered that perhaps he hadn't told my mother, that his appearance would be a surprise, that he didn't know it was graduation night. Instead of at school, he'd be waiting at the house, after our dinner at a restaurant."

Audiobook Reader
"Hear the loud alarum bells—
Brazen bells!"

Rob
[reading]
"This was false also."

Audiobook Reader
"How they clang, and clash, and roar!
What a horror they outpour
On the—"

Rob
[reading]
"I turned the dinner into a funeral; likewise the cake and presents at home. They all knew that something was wrong, inquired gently, saw I couldn't tell them, and tried to make the best of the evening. I headed upstairs, knowing they'd talk about me as soon as I'd left. I didn't care."

Audiobook Reader
"Hear the tolling of the bells—
Iron bells!"

Rob
[reading]
"I sat down. I felt empty, as if I'd fasted a week. I flipped on the radio. It was on AM, far down in the six hundreds. I stared at the illuminated dial. I saw it as something human, glared at it as the man in Poe's *The Tell-tale Heart* glared at his victim's hateful eye."

Audiobook Reader
"In the silence of the night,
How we shiver with affright
At the—"

Rob
[reading]
"I punched the Seek button. The tuner jumped to six-eighty."

5th Radio Announcer
—mowed down the Giants, thirteen strikeouts in—

Rob
[reading]
"I punched it again. It stopped at seven-forty."

1st Radio Announcer
—traffic and weather every ten minutes.

Rob
[reading]
"Again. Harder."

2nd Radio Announcer
—car insurance rates you can live with. In Redwood City, call Greg van—

Audiobook Reader
"—tolling, tolling,
In that muffled monotone—"

Rob
[reading]
"I kept hitting the button harder and harder—"

3rd Radio Announcer
—*por la comida mas sabrosa de*—

Rob
[reading]
"—over—"

4th Radio Announcer
—the Beach Boys doing "Good Vibrations."

Rob
[reading]
"—and over—"

5th Radio Announcer
—will steam clean all your carpets—

Audiobook Reader
"Keeping time, time, time
In a sort of Runic rhyme—"

Rob
[reading]
"—and over—"

Audiobook Reader
"To the throbbing of the bells—
Of the bells, bells, bells—"

1st Radio Announcer
On Wall Street, the Dow was up twenty-nine—

Rob
[reading]
"—and over—"

2nd Radio Announcer
—two free tickets to give away to the fifth caller—

Rob
[reading]
"—until I'd punched it—"

3rd Radio Announcer
—suing the big tobacco companies—

Audiobook Reader
"As he knells, knells, knells—"

4th Radio Announcer
—George Jones and Tammy Wynette singing—

Rob
[reading]
"—all the way—"

5th Radio Announcer
—save up to thirty percent—

Rob's Grandmother
"Oranges and lemons—"

1st Radio Announcer
—easy listening ninety-six point five.

Rob's Grandmother
"Say the bells of St. Clement's."

Rob
[reading]
"—to the very end of the dial."

Audiobook Reader
"To the rolling of the bells—
Of the bells, bells, bells—"

Boy Rob and Audiobook Reader
"To the tolling of the bells—
Of the bells, bells, bells, bells—"

Rob and Boy Rob and Audiobook Reader
"Bells, bells, bells—"

Rob
[reading]
"I was sick, sick, sick, sick, *sick* of seeking and never finding. I hit Seek one more time. It went back to the six hundreds."

2nd Radio Announcer
Coming up on the Giants postgame show—

Rob
[reading]
"I slammed my fist down on the radio, grabbed the cord, and yanked the plug out of the socket. The dial lost its light. I stared at it in triumph. And straight to its face I yelled out my birthday wish."

Boy Rob
I hope I never meet him!

Rob
[reading]
"Then—"

Boy Rob
And I'm through with radios!

[We hear the sound-effects recording. It begins fading out after half a minute, overlapping the following speech.]

Lenny
"Bus Stop" by the Hollies, 1966. Yes, indeed. Maybe the only song to explore the romantic possibilities of the umbrella. But it's wet in England, so I guess it figures. Kind of a cultural artifact. We do songs about yellow polka-dot bikinis, they do songs about rainwear. And public trans-portation. I mean a song about a bus stop—what a concept. How many zillions of songs have we written about cars? And how many can you name about buses, or BART, or AMTRAK? Well, then again, hold on a second. There was Duke Ellington. "Take the A Train." Sure enough. Which leads conveniently to our next caller.

3rd Female Caller
Hey, Lenny. Take me back to the thirties, OK? It's not like I was living back then, but that's where I want to go. Play me some Count Basie. I don't care what. Something snappy. Surprise me. And I just wanted to say that, sure there's hardship out there, and suffering, but you don't have to let it get you down. That's not the only reality. All the religions, every one of 'em, tell you there's another world behind this one. That's what religion is all about, getting you over to it. Getting you across the busy street,

with all the horns honking and distractions and accidents. But on the other side, there's harmony. That's where artists live. They're telling us about it. They don't listen to the depressing headlines on the news. They're busy listening to the Music of the Spheres. And writing down what it sounds like. And it's full of joy. And it might surprise some folks, but it's not church hymns, or requiems, or like that. The Music of the Spheres—I've studied up on it, so you can take it from me—it's Big Band music.

[We hear an up-tempo Count Basie instrumental. It begins fading out after half a minute, overlapping the following speech.]

1st and 2nd Students
[singing, to the tune in West Side Story]
"When you're a Jet
You're a Jet all the way
From—"

Female English Teacher
I don't believe this. Can't anyone in the class—I'll read it one last time. "She was wearing a sombrero *on her head* which came from Mexico." What's wrong with that sentence?

[Pause]

3rd Student
It really came from Guatemala?

Zad

You could always put in a legal disclaimer. "The opinions expressed about this school in the following work are not necessarily the author's, even though it's an autobiography."

Rob

Cute.

Coach

C'mon, men—cut the moaning and sighing! Chin-ups are easy! Give it all you've got! Show me a hundred and ten, a hundred and twenty percent! Winkler! How many was that?

4th Student

Three.

Coach

Was that giving a hundred and twenty percent?

4th Student

Actually, you can't really, I'm like taking precalculus, but we studied percentages back in fourth grade, and it's not like actually possible to give *more than* a hundred—

Coach

You're not in math class—you're in the gym! And in the gym it's possible! Now get back up there and pull!

Female English Teacher

"—wearing a sombrero *on her head which came from Mexico*." Did her head come from Mexico? Did she buy it for five pesos in the market? Did you all buy yours at the same stall?

Spanish TV Actress

Toda la noche, Rodrigo. Toda la noche me pregunto, ¿por qué? ¿Por qué? ¿Por qué?

Dean

—been a dean here a good long time, and believe me, you're not the first. We run into this every few years. A particular class comes in and thinks they can break all the rules. They want four strikes before they strike out. Special treatment. Just throw the rule book out the window. But I'm the ref around here. And let me tell you—

Rob

[reading]

"I was nervous about high school. My three best friends had taken the private-school exit. Jefferson looked like a battleship: huge, gray, a scarred survivor of a thousand vandal attacks. Two other unknown middle schools converged here, pouring strangers into the halls. I'd never gone to a school with security guards before. They lent the cafeteria that prison ambience so conducive to loss of appetite. After two days I begged my mother to let me home-school, but she—"

Mrs. Druckenmuller

A first-year reporter, as we know, is called a "cub." Let's welcome our three new cub reporters—Zad, Gloria, and Rob.

1st Student

The three bears.

2nd Student

Here, cubbie, cubbie, cubbie!

Mrs. Druckenmuller

Yes, Zad.

Zad

What I don't get is why we're the Jefferson Jets. I mean Thomas Jefferson believed in a country of small farmers, right? Which doesn't exactly go with jet planes.

Mrs. Druckenmuller

Well, I suppose—

3rd Student

What do you want—the Hicks?

4th Student

The Tillers?

3rd Student

I don't think the coaches would go for it.

Sports Editor

"Tillers Plow Berkeley Lady Hoopsters." Interesting.

1st Student

Or one of those singular names, like the Miami Heat.

2nd Student

The Manure.

Sports Editor

"Manure Smothers Pirates." I don't think so. Who cares what Jefferson thought? It's all about headlines on the sports page. "Jets Strafe Pirates." "Jets Bomb Palo Alto Back to Stone Age." "Jets Flush Toilet Over—"

Mrs. Druckenmuller

Thank you, Tony.

Rob's Mother

You remember that day, Rob? Here's the page. "March 4th. Bees among the almond blossoms, going door to door to door. Wings thrumming, stirring the scents in the air, mixing spring into winter. Batter: folding warm ingredients into cold." They're just images and ideas. At least that's what I use mine for. Not finished poems, but materials. Wood stacked next to a building site.

3rd and 4th Students
[singing]

"—you're a Jet all the way
From Coach Keppler's bad breath
To Miss Rourke's lingerie.
When you're a Jet you can—"

Rob
[reading]

"I'd put all my radio equipment in the attic that summer. I was no longer a DJ; I was a writer. My mother bought me a journal with a marbled cover. We began taking sketching trips, not to paint but to sketch scenes in words: the Sonoma vineyards, a video arcade, Muir Woods, Skid Row. We went to bookstore readings together. She let me sit in on her writing group—"

Female Writer

—that the publishers could steal your ideas, which is why I always put the copyright sign and the year on the title page, but just to be safer I put the month and the day, too, in case there's a dispute, and then under that I put "All Rights Reserved" in bold type, *underlined*—

Rob
[reading]

"—and she'd suggested I join the school paper. The *Jetstream* bore disappointingly little resemblance to the *Washington Post* in *All the President's Men.* The editorials had to be approved by Mrs. Druckenmuller, the dean, and the principal, and dealt with such hard-hitting issues as—"

1st Student
[reading]
"—even though they may be in a hurry, students must stop and realize that running, bumping, and even shoving each other has made our hallways nearly as dangerous as the freeways. We believe that it's time—"

Rob
How old is Mrs. Druckenmuller anyway?

Zad
I think she covered the Roosevelt inauguration. I'm speaking of Teddy.

Rob
I think she was already here when the Spanish arrived.

Zad
I think she was here when the Indians crossed the land bridge from Asia, *added Zad informatively*.

Mrs. Druckenmuller
Always try to spice up your stories with interesting verbs. Never use "said." "Said" puts readers to sleep

every time. I want you all to see what a fine job Jennifer did in her interview with the vice principal. *[Reading]* "'I've always enjoyed sports,' *he commented.* 'Before serving as vice principal, I coached the Jets' football and wrestling teams,' *he added thoughtfully.*" Now that's some fine, lively reporting.

Rob
[reading]

"October 8th. Driving back from Sierras, parked car to watch huge flock of swirling blackbirds. Flock dives unexpectedly like kite. Like flapping flag that's blown free from flagpole. Bends in half like blanket being folded and unfolded by invisible hands. Stretches like pizza dough. Morphs in air: living screen-saver. Sudden movements executed by all members simultaneously: marching band without drum major."

Zad

Where do I talk into? In·here? TESTING, TESTING, THIS IS ONLY A TEST. HAD THIS BEEN AN ACTUAL EMERGENCY YOU WOULD HAVE BEEN IN-STRUCTED TO COVER YOURSELF ALL OVER WITH TINFOIL. THEN PREHEAT YOUR OVEN TO FOUR HUNDRED DEGREES.

Rob's Grandfather

Such a waste. Ridiculous! There was immigration, drug laws, AIDS—

Rob's Grandmother

—the environment, First Amendment issues with the Internet. So many topics really worth tackling. I was proud of what you did.

Zad

My career on the *Jetstream*? How could I forget? Quite easily, actually, because my stories were totally forgettable, *he asserted factually*. Am I talking too loud into this? My first story, which actually was so short it had to be measured in column millimeters, was a riveting report on the decoration committee's new officers, a surprise announcement that precipitated mass suicides on campus—remember? I scooped the *Chronicle* on that one, I might add. That's the sort of stuff they gave us all year. The only sort of stuff they printed. All the news that's fit to ignore.

Rob

[reading]

"Like the *Jetstream*, high school in general wasn't what I'd expected. I'd imagined it as just a step below Stanford and Berkeley. Instead, it turned out to be run largely by former PE coaches, whose motivational and crowd-control skills apparently qualified them to become administrators. Order was the order of the day, not education. We were still being handed prefab worksheets from teacher guides. I had no inspiring teachers my first year. In class, Habit Bingo was a popular student pastime."

2nd Student
[whispering throughout scene]
See how she keeps touching her hair?

Rob

Yeah.

2nd Student
So every time she does, you get to fill in that square. Same with running her tongue over her front teeth, or staring at the Nathaniel Hawthorne poster.

Rob
What's that about, anyway?

2nd Student
Maybe she's got the hots for him. He's been dead for like hundreds of years, right?

Rob

Right.

2nd Student
She must have given up on the dating scene. Totally. Now look at my card. If she says the word "glean"—

Female English Teacher
Silas Marner, chapter seven. Who can tell me what you gleaned from—

2nd and 3rd Student
Bingo!

Rob
[reading]
"Mrs. Druckenmuller put emphasis on the traditions of journalism, such as typing the number thirty at the bottom of a story, ancient reporter code for 'the end.'"

Zad
She'd actually mark you off if you didn't. But I was so sick of our stupid, limp carrot of a newspaper that I typed a twenty-nine at the bottom. Which you saw. And the elevator started heading down.

Rob
Twenty-eight.

Zad
Twenty-seven.

Rob
Twenty-five and a half.

Zad
Eleven.

Rob
We were puny freshmen. Pretty amazing, really. This was like storming the Bastille. Open revolt. Druckenmuller gave us that lecture.

Zad

You said they were typos.

Rob

Then we switched to Roman numerals.

Zad

Then you thought up the equations that equaled thirty.

Rob

Two x plus five, times eighty over two—

Zad

—minus fourteen squared, divided by three—

Rob

It was the first time I'd gotten less than an "A" in behavior.

Zad

Late bloomer.

Rob's Grandmother

—so he moved to Seattle and got a job on the *Post-Intelligencer*, which promptly fired him for—

Rob

Wait a second. That's really the name of a paper?

Rob's Grandmother
The *Post-Intelligencer*. Crazy but true.

Rob
[reading]
"—seemed like the dumbest name imaginable for a paper. Which is actually what got me started—the name. It was just a joke. I made the first issue that night in my room: one side of a page, hand-written, with a hand-drawn nose at the top."

Zad
It's great! *The Jefferson Post-Nasal Drip*. "All the News That's Snot Fit to Be in the *Jetstream*."

Rob
But we basically forgot about it over the summer, right? Then we did the back-to-school issue—

Zad
—with reviews of teachers. Man, we were brutal.

Rob
They deserved it.

Zad
And then I showed it to Penelope—

Rob
—and she did the fall antifashion report.

Zad
And then things really started hopping.

Rob
[reading]
"The front page featured parodies of *Jetstream* stories, jabs at school and political figures, general irreverence. The back page had real news of interest to students: movie reviews, stories on minimum wage, ratings of Internet providers. We all worked on whatever interested us. As well as being a good writer, Penelope could draw— handy for altering photos of the student council, putting pig noses on the faces of public figures, etc. She had a scanner for graphics, two hundred fonts, and a good eye for design. By the middle of our sophomore year, we were printing thirty copies to pass out to friends. Then fifty. Then seventy-five. A sympathetic teacher got hold of one and slipped us three reams of paper. We went to four pages, single-sided. Then we added a fifth, a supplement called 'The Sneeze.'"

Penelope
Remember the free ads for stores we liked? "We accept no money for these advertisements."

Penelope and Rob's Grandfather
"The *Drip* can be read, but never bought."

Rob's Grandfather
Hey   that's my boy. Give 'em hell, Robbie.

Rob's Mother

My favorite? Well, I thought "Dear Flabby" was brilliant—the thin girls writing in wanting to gain weight because no one will look at a girl under two hundred pounds. The recipes for coconut milk éclairs, deep-fried éclairs, Spam-filled éclairs. And I was a big "Ann Philanders" fan, of course.

Penelope
[reading]

"Dear Confused Sophomore: I've gone through the entire Bible—and guess what? There's absolutely *nothing* prohibiting sex with a computer science teacher. So relax and enjoy. He sounds like a wonderful man. If it doesn't work out, maybe you'd be kind enough to give him my—"

Rob's Grandfather

—the story you did on Thomas Jefferson's half-black children. That was a strong piece of writing. You really took the gloves off.

Rob's Grandmother

And then the letter to the editor, *signed by Grandpa*—

Rob's Grandfather
[reading]

"—propose that, beginning next fall, the Jefferson team name be changed to the Mulattos." *The Mulattos*?

Rob's Grandmother
The one time he got a letter printed—and he didn't write it.

Penelope
That was the best part. When it was really spreading, but most of the school didn't know who was writing it. It was the big mystery on campus. Talk about buzz. We really *could* have sold ads—big time.

Zad
My favorite, personally, was the tabloid issue. With the front page Penelope did up exactly like the *National Enquirer*.

Rob
"Piece of the Cross Found in Jefferson Woodshop."

Zad
"DNA Tests Reveal Entire Cafeteria Staff from Distant Galaxy."

Penelope
The teachers were giving us probing looks, wondering who was behind it. Then somebody let the cat out of the bag. Which made us even bigger heroes.

Dean
So you admit that you're responsible for this publication?

Zad

Yep.

Dean

And I suppose that you know how to read?

Rob

Fairly obvious.

Dean

You can cut the flippancy right there. I want you to do me a little reading aloud. Start with that paragraph, from the California Education Code. The section on student publications.

Zad

It was sort of a badge of honor, being called in to the dean's office.

Penelope

We sure got ourselves a big badge collection.

Rob

[reading]

"The administration didn't know what to do with us. There hadn't been an underground paper on campus since the seventies. They tried to shut us down, which naturally made us persecuted victims, which naturally raised readership three hundred percent. Then they got smart. They ignored us. We were allowed to distribute the paper off school grounds. After a while, it didn't seem funny anymore."

Zad

It was like—we've done that already. Let's do something new, less jokey. So we started the campaigns.

Penelope

It's a simple question, really. I would just like to know how much money Jefferson receives from the Coca-Cola Corporation in return for Coke being the only soft drink available on campus.

Rob

So you're saying that you can't tell me for a fact that our gym clothes weren't made in sweatshops?

Zad

Since everybody knows too much fat and salt are bad, I guess I'd just like to hear why it is that McDonald's food is in our cafeteria.

Rob

[reading]

"We changed the name from the *Drip* to *El Grito*— the shout. The paper came in handy for getting our message across. We were like cattle dogs, constantly nipping at them. Sometimes we drew blood. I did a fake interview with the vice principal in one issue, complete with Penelope's doctored photos of him shaking hands with Hitler and eating piles of McDonald's hamburgers while starving Africans watched through the window. He probably could have sued us. Instead, he suddenly retired at semester break. Through the door that connected our two halves of the house, I heard my mother and grandparents—"

Rob's Grandfather
—at Lenny. And what's wrong with him channeling it into that? He's running an underground paper, not stealing cars. He's found himself some fine substitutes to attack. Who was out with the ropes and crowbars, tearing down the statues of Lenin all over Europe? Men who hate their fathers, that's who.

Rob
[reading]
"My ears rang. The hairs on my head straightened. I knew he was right. I tiptoed away, not wanting to hear more."

Rob's Mother
Yes, I do have a new one to read. It's untitled, at this point.
"On your fingertips:
fresh-sawn Douglas fir,
sawdust and plasterdust
squeezed under your nails—"

Rob
[reading]
"My grandfather's words had hit the mark, but didn't lead me to sound the retreat. It was something

else entirely that caused that to happen."

Rob's Mother
"Sap stains dark as birthmarks,
potent as smelling salts:
the scent of new rooms—"

Rob
[reading]
"When my mother finally couldn't stand our old
kitchen cabinets another minute, she had a carpenter
put in new ones. The cabinet job seemed to lead to
others. The carpenter always read a book while he ate
lunch in his truck. My mother noticed this and they
started talking books. His name was Andrew. Then he
became Andy."

Zad
Did you ever notice how everyone picked
boyfriends or girlfriends from the other middle
schools. It was like we were tired of the same old faces.

Rob
Mick and Christa.

Zad
Penelope and Sean.

Rob
The lure of the exotic.

Zad
Like Mr. Wirtz was saying in biology. It's exogamy.

Rob's Grandmother
[reading]
"Exogamy: Marrying outside one's family, tribe, or social unit."

Rob
[reading]
"I saw this in my mother as well. Andy was a reader, but spent most of his life working with wood, not words. And he was blond, as no one in my family was. And he liked to read fantasy—"

Andy
[reading]
"—had vowed never to submit to the tyrannical rule of Gunthor, whose armies, captained by his half-brother Ogrit, had spread terror throughout Valandria, just as the seer Simso had predicted before he'd been slain by Gunthor's uncle, Heffelvorp—"

Rob
[reading]
"—a genre utterly unrepresented on our many bookshelves."

Tango Teacher
Left, right, pivot, right, back, three, four, pivot—

Rob's Mother

You were never an albatross around my neck. Never.

Rob

But it's not like you see singles ads out there that say "Desperately seeking woman with messy, night-owl, picky-eating son who will sabotage any relationship."

Rob's Mother

Well, no. But then again, you scared off that tango teacher from Argentina. Thank God.

Tango Teacher

¿Nunca duerme tu hijo?

Boy Rob

I know what you're saying. "Don't I go to sleep?" No, I don't. And I like tango music. And I'm going to stay up and watch you guys.

Penelope

"Dear Ann Philanders: There's a guy I like whom I'll call Pope Julius II (not his real name). I've tried every line in *The Seven Surefire Come-ons of Highly Effective Pickup Artists, Scoring for Dummies, Scoring for Idiots, Reproduction for Dummies,* but nothing has worked. How can I hook him?"

"Dear Desperate: It seems pretty clear that you just aren't his taste in bait. Take the hint. And if you wouldn't mind passing him my number and photo—"

Rob's Mother
[reading]
"On my fingertips:
minced garlic, shallots,
shrimp, red pepper,
a scale model of dinner—"

Spanish TV Actor
Es una persona de confianza.

Andy
A person—

Rob's Mother
Someone we can trust.

Spanish TV Actor
Nos encontrará aquí a las nueve.

Andy
I got "nine o'clock."

Rob's Mother
She'll meet us here at nine o'clock. Good.

Rob
[reading]
"My mother had had boyfriends over the years,
but nothing long-lasting or serious, at least as far as I

knew. But Andy not only took my mother to movies, he came to dinners with my grandparents, then back-packing in the Sierras with us that summer. We got call waiting—ostensibly for me, since my friends were calling all the time—but really for my mother. From the poems she read to the writing group, I knew this was serious, and that she wanted me to know that it was. He was cheery, a whistler, but otherwise quieter than anyone in my family. I think we were all impressed by someone who didn't feel the need to constantly tell the world everything he was thinking. He'd been married long before, had no children but did have a black retriever, a dog who—"

Boy Rob

But I just wanted to pet it.

Rob's Grandmother

But the dog doesn't know you. That's why it growled. Never go up and pet a dog you don't know. Hold out your hand and let it come to you if it wants to.

Rob
[reading]

"Andy followed that advice with me. No shoving a football in my arms and leading me to the street. No expensive gift on my birthday. He loved cribbage, brought over a cribbage board he'd made, taught my mother to play, but never corralled me. He was pleasant, patient, easy to be around. Yet something in me wouldn't let me go to his hand."

Rob's Mother
We're gonna walk down and get some ice cream.

Rob
"We. Pronoun. Plural. Specifically, Rob and Rose Radkovitz."

Rob's Mother
You want to come along, Rob?

Rob
[reading]
"The same dictionary still sat on our stand, but somehow the definition had changed. My mother and I had always been like two binary stars, revolving around each other. We shared each other's interests to an unusual degree, always ate dinner together, always looked forward to it. She taught, had meetings with parents, had friends, but I knew I came first. In a way, we were like spouses. And in a way, I began feeling I was being divorced."

Rob's Mother
Robbie—did you hear? June had the baby!

Rob's Grandmother
I'll put the presents in the car.

Rob's Mother
It's a girl! You've got a cousin!

Rob

Hey, that's great. I've also got an overdue history research paper.

Aunt June

Well, you were a teenager. A teenaged boy. Boys don't usually go crazy over babies. I forgave you, Robbie. You'd been the only kid and only grandkid for so long that—

Rob
[reading]

"February 12th. Visiting June in hospital. Imagining baby is me, June my mother: So this is what that scene was like, what I looked like. Yet this was also a chance to be there as an adult. Two-point perspective."

Aunt Jessica

She's so perfect, June! Look at you two! Nick's coming over right after work. I want him to see. He hasn't ruled out adoption, but he wants some time. So I bought him a hamster. To get him used to taking care of something. After that, I thought maybe a kitten.

Rob's Grandmother

A hamster?

Jessica

Is that moving too fast?

Rob's Grandfather
I think you better back up. Maybe a rock collection.
Coins. Something that doesn't eat.

Rob
[reading]
"I knew I should have been overjoyed for Aunt
June. She'd waited so long, first to find a husband,
then to have a baby. Just as my mother had waited so
long—"

Mr. McCarthy
Think of your autobiography as a letter addressed
to your future self, to someone who only faintly
remembers what—

Rob
And whenever she's with him, they're always
laughing. It's weird.

Zad
The exact same with my mom last year. It's a stage
they go through.

Rob
What's to laugh about when you're doing the
dishes?

Zad
Or hiking up some monster trail in the sun?

Rob

Last night they went to this lecture by some guy who'd been tortured in Argentina.

Zad

Probably laughed their heads off.

Rob
[reading]

"They went on tours of historic houses. They made dinners together. They went to concerts. I was secretly pleased that he didn't like opera. It was the one realm he'd left me. I made a New Year's resolution that year to work my way through all of Verdi."

Rob's Mother

But we're trying to watch TV, Rob.

Rob

But the acoustics are so much better here. C'mon!

Spanish TV Actress
Nunca te voy a dar la foto. ¡Nunca!

Rob
[reading]

"Andy was trying to learn Spanish. His accent was hopeless. Vocabulary was also a problem. We three went to a Mexican restaurant—"

Andy

What's she laughing about? I asked her to put it in a doggie bag, right? *Un saco de perro.*

Rob's Mother

Sweetie. You were trying your best. It's just dangerous, translating literally.

Andy

So what did I say?

Rob's Mother

You don't want to know.

Andy

Actually, I do.

Rob's Mother

Well, you—you asked her to put the food in a—in a—in a dog's scrotum.

Rob
[reading]

"I laughed at him, too loudly I knew. He laughed at himself. My mother laughed with the waitress till she cried."

Rob's Grandmother

It's from Mrs. Kathos. For you, Robbie. The moving van came this morning.

Rob
[reading]

"After Mr. Kathos next door died, his wife began to decline and had to move to a nursing home. She'd made one last batch of baklava for all the neighbors. I stared at the piece on the paper plate. The smell took me right back to being a kid—"

Lenny
Makes your wallpaper change right there on the wall to what you had when you were a baby—

Mrs. Kathos
That's enough sweeping, Robbie. You sit now and eat.

Rob
[reading]

"March 22nd. Last piece of baklava. Scent of honey, lemon, nuts. Staring at my sweet, pampered childhood. Last remaining square. Didn't want to eat it."

Penelope
A dog's scrotum? Oh, my God. And they're still together?

Rob
Yeah.

Penelope

Then it's serious. That's definitely one of the ten warning signs. I read it in Ann Philanders.

Rob
[reading]

"They took me to things they thought would interest me. I was a mannequin in the car, a deaf-mute when we got there, a vanishing spirit when we returned. I knew I was being childish, churlish, uncharitable, unfair, but I couldn't stop myself. I was in a riptide, and couldn't swim out of it."

Rob's Mother

I'd tried talking to you, in a roundabout way, but it wasn't helping. You were listening on some other frequency. I had to find it. When I did, I decided to be direct.

Rob
[reading]

"I was listening to opera. It was night. She slowly turned down the volume. Then she turned it off. Then she turned off all the lights one by one. Then she sat down in the rocker. Then, in the dark, she said—"

Rob's Mother

Tell me everything you're afraid of.

Rob
[reading]

"'Tell me everything you're afraid of.' I was lying on the couch. I turned my face away from her, toward the cushions. Then I started crying. Started, and couldn't stop. She came over, kneeled beside me, and lay her head on my back a long time. Then she stretched out next to me on the couch and held me, arms around me like a life preserver. She held me that way until past midnight."

Penelope
[reading]

"Dear Unsure in Oakland: The new guy your mom is going out with, whom I'll call Krevkor, Son of Borf (not his real name), sounds well-built and fabulously rich but has some issues that require professional evaluation. I've enclosed my card, so he can set up an appointment, along with a recent photo (up-to-date except for bangs trim and frosting two weeks ago)—"

Rob
[reading]

"The next night, we had a talk. I started out with the big stuff, and got down to things like his yogurts filling up the door shelf in the fridge and who sits where at the dinner table, things she hadn't known bothered me. It took hours until I couldn't find anything else to bring up. But then the barrel was finally empty. I felt drained, and better. And then we slept—thirteen hours in my case. And then, a few days later, Andy came over for dinner. I sat at my old place at the table. A week or two after that, I asked him to teach me how to play cribbage."

[We hear the sound-effects recording. It begins fading out after half a minute, overlapping the following speech.]

4th Female Caller
So then I found out he wasn't just seeing another woman, but women, plural, extremely plural, and I just felt really used and deceived, and it's taking a really long time to get over it, but I hope he's listening tonight, 'cause I'd like you to find the soundtrack to South Pacific, *which my sisters and I listened to all the time when we were kids. Those songs really stay with you forever, and I'd like you to play that song on there, "I'm Gonna Wash That Man Right Outa My Hair" and I'd like you to play it really loud.*

Lenny
Whoa, hold on a minute. Down, girl. I mean, washing him out of your hair's probably a good idea, and then maybe a hundred strokes with one of those wire brushes you get at the hardware store, just to make sure he's gone. But this show's here to celebrate the past, not trash it. So try one of the other stations. Or maybe you should make him a tape. That song you asked for, then "Your Cheatin' Heart," then "Seven Beers with the Wrong Man"—you'd definitely want a sixty-minute tape. Maybe a ninety. Or drop the big one on him and give him a whole hundred and

twenty minutes of righteous accusation, not available in stores or catalogs, with all your all-time favorite guilt-inducing hits by Tammy Wynette, Aretha Franklin, Helen Reddy, Maria Callas, Big Mama Thornton, and many others, order now and receive at no extra charge—actually, let's get on to our next caller.

3rd Male Caller
Yeah, would you play "Bésame Mucho" by Trio Los Panchos. I don't really want to discuss it. Thanks.

Lenny
Hey, I'm not here to pry. You want "Bésame Mucho"? Fine by me. Lo que sea, like my old lady used to say. That's Spanish for "whatever." So without further ado—

Spanish TV Actor
Siempre recuerdes.

Andy
Always—

Rob's Mother
—remember—

Spanish TV Actor
Te adoro.

Andy
I adore you.

Spanish TV Actress

Te adoro.

Rob's Mother

I adore you.

Andy

I adore you.

Rob's Mother

Are you translating, or telling me something.

Andy

Telling you something. For extra credit.

Mr. McCarthy

Do the writers tell you everything? Every burp and sneeze? Of course not. They pick and choose. Which I hope you're doing as well. *Nothing over a thousand pages, please.*

Rob's Mother

That was how I knew.

Rob's Grandmother

When you made the bed together?

Rob's Mother

You see how sensitive the other person is to your movements. If you speed up or slow down to match each other. If you communicate well without words.

How patient you both are. How much or little detail matters—smoothing out wrinkles, folding back the bedspread. If another's help is a joy or creates conflict. For us, it was always this lovely duet. It's a tango, without touching.

Rob's Grandmother
Your father's never made the bed in fifty-seven years.

Rob's Grandfather
Sorry, but the back doctor told me, "No tangos."

Rob
[reading]
"My mother and Andy got married in Golden Gate Park. She took his last name—Allston. I remained a Radkovitz and felt as though I were watching her depart on a train, leaving the family name behind."

Rob's Mother
"Strange that on the day we'd decided
I found myself watering the lemon tree,
a green plastic pitcher in each hand—"

Rob
[reading]
"Andy, his furniture, his large dog Marco, his yoga exercises, his talk radio stations, his chili recipe, his long baths, etc., entered our two-bedroom, one-bathroom home. It was like trying to squeeze—"

Rob

What do you think of the sign?

Rob's Mother

"Mother of All Garage Sales." Great. But now it's time to live up to it. I'm getting rid of three whole boxes of books. You've got a bunch you haven't read in years, up here and downstairs, that really ought to—

Rob

I already went through all my books.

Rob's Mother

And?

Rob

And—I'm selling those.

Rob's Mother

Five books? Rob, honey, come on. Let's look through them together. Look, right here. *Our Forest Friends.* From preschool days. Do you still need that?

Rob

I might. You never know.

Mr. McCarthy

Your life's too ordinary? Think back to what we've read this year—*Black Boy,* Isabel Allende, *This Boy's Life.*

Rob's Mother
"—watching the streams meet in midair,
slicing through and sliding over each other—"

Neva
So are you going to write about me?

Rob
We're not supposed to tell McCarthy everything.
Remember? But I thought maybe a cryptic dedication.
Am I in yours?

Neva
You've got a few numbers after your name in the
index.

Rob
If you help me with chemistry I'll put you in the
acknowledgments. "Without whose advice, support,
and incredibly beautiful eyes—"

Andy
OK. You're doing great behind the wheel, Rob. So
now let's try some bigger hills. Are you up for
Lombard?

Zad
He took you on Lombard? The Mother of All
Hills?

Rob

I swear, this is why my mom got married, just so she could have someone else teach me to drive.

Penelope

Most marriage counselors don't consider that a good enough reason.

Zad

Ann Philanders says there's gotta be more.

Penelope

Like a cute butt, for one.

Rob

Would you guys shut up? So we survive Lombard, which is fun—you should try it. Then we're on Van Ness and he says how you have to learn to tune out distractions. So he turns on the radio to a talk station.

1st Radio Announcer

—because the self-appointed liberal, humanist high priests who *probably are* descended from monkeys—

Rob

And then he's got a boom box running on batteries in the backseat, and he turns that on, and it's Sunday, and it's tuned to some gospel show.

2nd Radio Announcer

—that we praise Him in the morning! Not just

Sunday morning, but every day, when the light rises in the east!

1st Radio Announcer
—fluoride in the water and Darwinism in the schools—

Rob
And then he whips out a harmonica and starts honking away on *that*—

2nd Radio Announcer
Praise Him without ceasing!

Rob
—beating time with his feet as loud as he can, and I'm completely cracking up, trying to stay in my lane—

Zad
And you lived?

Rob's Mother
"—the waters merging, braiding, embracing—"

Rob
[reading]
"August 23rd. Andy's entrance: house molts, new plumage. Different couch and coffee table. New knick-knacks on my mother's bookshelf unattached to any memories of mine. Marco sheds, digs, howls if left alone. Blended family: my stepbrother is a dog. Andy

calm during freeway driving lessons; medication? Beat him at cribbage last night. His chili not bad."

Andy

Seconds anyone?

Rob

For me, actually. Thanks.

Andy

And can I put that in a dog's scrotum for you?

Rob

Please.

Andy

At your service.

Rob

Gracias.

Andy

De nada.

Rob

[reading]

"Junior year was given to *El Grito,* swing dance music, Russian novels, making films on the computer, Beethoven, and writing. The next summer I began learning some yoga from Andy—breathing exercises, simple positions. You're supposed to clear your mind of thoughts, but one night I was in the fallen leaf position on the living room rug, while my mother graded papers and Andy brushed the dog, and the thought struck me out of nowhere: My real father wasn't coming back. And then: I don't really mind. I felt muscles, bones, joints, ligaments all relax, go slowly and utterly slack. I felt like a marionette who'd been laid on the floor. I closed my eyes, breathing in and breathing out. To me, this felt like Nirvana, the state that yoga masters spend lifetimes searching for."

Mr. McCarthy
Does it take an unusual, extraordinary life to make a compelling autobiography?

Rob
[reading]
"Andy's arrival had brought this about. He was up whistling in the kitchen every morning, walked the dog every night, took a long bath every Friday. He'd been living with us a year, and in the picture for the two before. He felt reliable and permanent: oak, not pine. I could sight down his and my mother's life as I could down one of those straight Central Valley roads. Lenny was nowhere in that picture. It was as if that whole issue had snapped shut, like a box. I heard the click of the clasp in that moment on the floor, and suddenly I knew that I could put that box up in the attic and stop looking at it. Which is exactly what I did in

my mind. I was still in the fallen leaf position. Eyes closed, I imagined myself getting a cardboard box and putting inside it the framed photo of Lenny, the oldies show tape, the sound-effects record, and my Louisiana school reports. I taped it shut. Then I pictured getting the ladder from the back porch, hauling it up the stairs, climbing it, opening the trapdoor, pulling the light-chain, and crawling into the attic with the box. I walked into the corner and set the box down next to the trunk. I stepped back and stared at it. Then another revelation struck: I could give up boycotting radio. It no longer mattered that Lenny had been a DJ. I wouldn't be imitating him or searching for him. All that was in the past. I no longer had any expectations about him. He was a moth I'd released into the night. I was beyond trying to catch him."

Rob's Grandmother
My, yes. It's an old classic song. "I Get Along Without You Very Well." Hoagy Carmichael, wasn't it?

Rob
[reading]
"I let this thought reverberate. I pictured myself turning, finding my shortwave, crouching down, blowing off the dust. When I backed down the ladder, I had it in my arms. Then I went back up and got my amp and speaker. I left this guided fantasy and opened my eyes. Slowly, I unfolded myself from the fallen leaf. I stood up. Then I did everything I'd just imagined."

3rd Radio Announcer
Eight-nine-four Benson Street. Ten-seventeen.

4th Radio Announcer
—reports excellent reception on his Grundig portable and writes that his favorite program is "Sweden Today."

Neva
I didn't know anything about you. I'd just moved here. I couldn't believe school started in early August, or that August could be as cold as winter in Chicago. I was in a bad mood. I remember seeing you that first day in English and you were reading some electronics magazine. And from that one detail I assumed you were a nerd and crossed you off my list—for three days, anyway.

Zad
Check it out. It's a wireless FM mike. Got it for my birthday.

Opera Radio Host
—from Kenosha, Wisconsin, has sent a question she hopes will stump our Opera Quiz panel. "Lohengrin," she writes, "makes his famous entrance in a boat pulled by a swan. But large freshwater birds have played a part in a number of other operas. Listen to the following—"

Rob
[reading]

"*El Grito* had gradually ground to a halt during eleventh grade. Our campaigns had fizzled out for the most part and my mind had been increasingly elsewhere. It was good to have radio back in my life that summer and to—"

Zad

You talk into the mike and your voice comes out on the radio.

Rob

Come on!

Zad

I'm serious. But it only works for like a radius of a hundred feet. So basically, you're broadcasting to your house. "Traffic moving well in the kitchen and den areas, with a report of cat vomit on the living room rug." Could be a public service sort of thing.

3rd Radio Announcer

—tonight's Giants payoff inning, in which players bat for you, the fans. Who's our first lucky listener?

4th Radio Announcer

Let's see here. Jesus—

Rob and Andy

Hay-ZOOSE!

4th Radio Announcer

—MAN-u-el.

Rob and Andy

Man-WELL!

Rob

God, it's so true. When I walk Marco, other people with dogs *wave at me*. I'm not a dog person, but they assume I am just because I've got a dog.

Neva

And last night when we were walking him together, and that couple with the stroller said "Hi" to us. It was dark, so they couldn't see us that well and I was thinking they probably thought we were older, like them, married, walking our dog.

Rob

Heading back to our apartment with the his and her bathroom sinks, our two BMWs in the garage, the hot tub on the deck.

Neva

Could we sell one of the BMWs so we could go to that writing workshop in Vermont?

5th Radio Announcer
—a low of fifty-eight tonight in Wichita, sixty-one in Hutchinson—

1st Radio Announcer
—tuned to the Night Owl on Radio Canada International.

Rob
[reading]
"We experimented with Zad's FM mike, setting radios to the right frequency and nonchalantly turning them on when our audience was near. Poetry readings on KMOM for my mother; station WOOD for Andy, featuring the wood price report; WORK, the Voice of Labor, for my grandfather, who'd broken his ankle and was in bed for weeks."

Zad
Next on WORK, a program of prison work songs, recorded live and in concert somewhere along Alabama's Highway Fifty-two. We know you'll want to get up and move around when you hear these, so don't hold back.

Rob's Grandfather
I can hardly wait! Someone get me a sledgehammer!

Rob

[reading]

"Family radio was a road I'd already traveled. I was looking for something larger in scope. 'Chance favors the prepared mind.' I was standing in line in a bagel shop, picked a *Chronicle* off a table, scanned the page it was folded to—and there was an article on pirate radio."

2nd Radio Announcer

—because the government's afraid, obviously, which you see in the news every day if you read between the lines, 'cause what it comes down to is they're afraid of the people, real people, not billionaire CEOs, so it's actually, I mean the Founding Fathers didn't really, they were afraid of democracy, they called the people "the mob," not like the Mafia, but, you know, like a crowd of—

Rob

Check out the names. Radio Chaos International. Radio Garbanzo.

Zad

KMUD.

Rob

Radio Free Texas.

                    Zad
The Voice of Laryngitis.

                    Rob
The Voice of Stench.

                    Zad
The Voice of Stench?

                    Rob
Now *that* is cool. We gotta hear that one.

                    Rob
                  [reading]
"I did some research. Finding pirate stations on the
dial turned out to be much harder than reading about
them. They change frequencies, broadcast irregularly,
drop out for months or years, get shut down. The only
one I found at first was giving a three-hour rant about
the FCC that eventually made me hungry for car clear-
ance sale ads."

            2nd Radio Announcer
—going to read you another article from the *Tom
Paine Review*, from a few years ago actually, about the
FCC-FBI-IRS connection, and the totally illegal seizure
of equipment from a guy who's like broadcasting from
his houseboat, right, on some little lake in Minnesota.
How did they ever find this guy, you ask? I mean
there's ten thousand lakes in Minnesota, right? That's

what it says on the license plate, anyway. Or is that Wisconsin? "The Show Me State." Hold on. That's Missouri. "Land of Lincoln." That's either Indiana or the other one—Illinois. Hell, let's look it up. I've got an almanac—no, it's in the house. Well, I'm getting hungry anyway. Suppose there's any of those noodles left? Man, there better be. You all just sit tight while Captain Kidd takes a little jaunt—

Zad

Two thoughts. Choosing our own radio names would be fun. And two—we can do better than this guy.

Rob

A girl named Neva? Of course I was intrigued. I'd been reading Russian novels and the Neva River was always cropping up. Coaches rattling into St. Petersburg and crossing the Neva, people drowning in it, characters standing on bridges and staring down at it.

Neva

No wonder you kept looking at me.

Rob

And the next thing I knew, we were reading E. E. Cummings love poems together. It all happened so fast.

Neva

"your little voice

Over the wires came leaping
and I felt suddenly
dizzy
With the jostling and shouting of merry flowers—"

Rob

God, that incredible rush when I'd pick up the phone and hear your voice.

Ray

Haven't seen you in a while. Or maybe I have but you grew so much I didn't know it was you. What can I do for you, my friend?

Rob
[reading]

"We pooled our money and bought a three-watt FM transmitter from Ray. He threw in a used mixing board for fifty dollars and helped us make a quarter-wave antenna out of some scrounged tubing. We got the antenna affixed to the pitched roof above my bedroom in a mere three hours and without attracting more than eight or so spectators waiting to see us plunge to our deaths, one of whom was filming us hopefully. That night we did a thirty-second test broadcast after midnight, me listening and recording in the living room while Zad—"

Zad

This is KPOW, Ka-pow, your anarchist alternative, signing on and signing off. It's been great, and you've been a terrific audience.

Rob

It worked! I could hear it!

Zad

Let me hear!

Rob

Gotta rewind.

Zad

This is KPOW, Ka-pow, your anarchist alternative—

Neva

"—floating hands were laid upon me
I was whirled and tossed into delicious dancing—"

Rob
[reading]

"September 10th. She's a river: long limbs, long black hair. Mystery of her source: the Midwest, unknown to me. Plays flute, bubbling source of rivers of music. Has read even more books than I have. Contemplating touching her, like a bather standing on a rock, afraid to jump in."

Zad

This is KPOW, Ka-pow, your anarchist alternative.
. . . This is KPOW—

Rob

[reading]

"After savoring our initial broadcast, the thrill of being on the airwaves was replaced by the awareness that we needed material worth broadcasting. Instead of smiting the system, I wanted to do something focused on writing. James, who'd been with us on *El Grito*, wanted to deal with issues beyond the bounds of high school. Zad—"

Zad

—as we listen to this great skit from the very first Monty Python record, which is incredibly rare, and has this—

James

—because people don't want to deal with homelessness anymore. They're tired of the issue. For them, it's like some TV show on endless reruns—

Rob

—will be reading her poetry this Saturday at City Lights, from two to three-thirty. So let's give you a preview—

Penelope
—incredible CDs from two new techno groups from Germany—

Rob
[reading]
"For our sign-on, we used a recording of an explosion from my old sound-effects CD. For sign-off, we taped the song "We'll Meet Again" from the video of *Dr. Strangelove*, which comes on at the end of the movie when all the nuclear bombs are going off. I covered the literature beat and took the name Radio Boy, which contained the letters R-O-B. Zad became Z-Man and did comedy, a traditional pirate radio category. A little later Neva joined in, interviewing neighborhood characters."

Neva
Exactly. Radio by the neighborhood, for the neighborhood. So you were saying that you worked down the hill in the shipyards. That must have really been an interesting time.

Old Man
What's that?

Neva
[loudly, as to someone hard of hearing]
You worked in the shipyards.

Old Man

I said that?

Neva

Yesterday, when we were talking.

Old Man

Yesterday . . . but I've never seen you before.

Neva

Remember? You were saying how you helped build ships during the war. And how women were working down there for the first time.

Old Man

Hmmm. Well, if you say so. Maybe I did, now that you mention it.

Rob

Oh, well. Not quite ready for prime-time pirate radio. You ought to interview my grandfather. He knows all about—

Zad

Yes, it was tuned in. And the sound was pathetic. And I only live ten blocks away.

Rob
[reading]
"September 25th. Mystery of radio: Only know

your voice going out, can't know who's hearing it. Conversation through a wall: neither side can see other. Radio listeners are voyeurs: lurking, invisible, eavesdropping. Broadcasters the opposite: You're onstage, but can't see who's in audience. Auditorium: a place for listening. With radio, seats sprinkled around city, listeners have no idea of seatmates. In our case, auditorium empty?"

Aunt June

Sorry, Robbie. Couldn't hear a thing. I had it tuned right where you said.

Neva

"How i was crazy how i cried when i heard
over time
and tide and death
leaping
Sweetly
your voice."

Rob

[reading]

"On the one hand, we didn't have to worry about the FCC or getting reported for interfering with other stations. On the other hand, no one was hearing us. We passed the collection plate among the pirate crew, went back to Ray, and bought a limiter, which was supposed to increase our range to several miles. Andy and I went out driving to see where we—"

Rob's Grandfather
It was the biggest general strike in American history.

Andy
Hey, there it is! It's Gramps on the air! Check the tripmeter.

Rob
Four point two miles.

Neva
And you still remember it?

Rob's Grandfather
I was only six, but I knew something was up. My father worked for the longshoremen's union—

Zad
This is KPOW—
[sound of explosion]
—your anarchist alternative, with the Z-Man at the pirate helm, bringing you what nobody else will play: weird British comedy from the group Beyond the Fringe—

Neva
You were the only boy I'd ever met who'd read *Pride and Prejudice* more than once.

Rob

And you were the only girl I'd ever met who's named after a Russian river, who can play the Bach unaccompanied flute sonata, and whose top ten book list had more than one book from mine—*War and Peace* and *Scrambled Eggs Super!*

Neva

I was just lucky I got you before Ann Philanders did.

Zad

—comedy that's so fast and so British you have *no clue* what's actually happening.

Rob

[reading]

"We only broadcast an hour or two at a time, with no set schedule. Out of paranoia about being discovered, we'd only told friends about the station, and yet we wanted to expand our audience and be heard by more than a few high-school students. We put up an inconspicuous card on a couple of record-shop bulletin boards with our call letters and frequency. We were so hungry to know that we were really out there and being listened to that we then went a step further: We announced my number over the air and asked listeners to call in with feedback. Penelope printed up QSL cards to mail out. We waited. Three broadcasts passed.

Then four. Not a single call from a stranger came in. We began almost to hope that at least the FCC was listening."

Zad

It's not like we're interfering with some megastation. No way they'd fine us.

Penelope

The worst they'd probably do is take away the equipment.

Zad

And kill themselves getting the antenna off the roof.

Penelope

And maybe give Rob a misdemeanor on his police record.

Zad

Which would maybe keep him from getting into college.

Penelope

Possibly leading to a life sentence to Burger King.

Zad

Depression, drinking, then drugs, then prime-time television watching—

Rob
[reading]

"Holidays are peak times for radio pirates, on the theory that FCC spies are on vacation like everybody else. And of all the holidays in the pirate radio year, Halloween is probably number one. We decided to join the fun and do five straight hours, which is taking a chance, beginning at ten. It was a Saturday. Everyone came over and Zad kicked us off with some old Firesign Theatre. We gave the phone number and asked listeners to call in. Friends started phoning and said reception was strong. Penelope played music for a while. James did a long piece on the sweatshops down on Third Street. I read a lot of E. E. Cummings, Pinsky, Borges, Rimbaud. Neva had just started reading from *Frankenstein*—"

Penelope

The phone rang again. You were busy, so Zad grabbed it. I looked at his face and I knew something was up. I could tell it wasn't one of our friends. And then it hit me: the FCC. These guys aren't stupid. They know pirates come out on Halloween.

Zad

First, he said he really liked the show. He was way too old to be someone from school. Then he said his name was Agent something or other. He asked if I wanted a corner prison cell or an aisle. Then he laughed. Then he asked for you.

Rob
[reading]
"It was too noisy, with everyone in the room. My parents had gone up the coast overnight, so I took the call in their room. The guy said that I had a good radio voice. I remember being impressed with myself."

Neva
"your little voice over the wires came leaping—"

Rob
[reading]
"He actually sounded familiar himself."

Lenny
And I'm not saying that just because I'm your father.

Rob
[reading]
"I was struck voiceless. A bell without a tongue. I shut the door and lay down on the bed. There was booming silence on the line."

Lenny
I've been visiting back out here for a week. First time in a long time. I know this is kind of a surprise.

Rob
[reading]
"When there's a flood on the news, you see strange groupings of objects going downstream together: a car, a doll, a whole tree. My mind was flooding. I heard my mother, a Monty Python skit, the Louisiana sound-effects record—"

[The sound-effects recording rises into hearing and plays behind the following speeches.]

Lenny
So I thought I'd give you a call. Believe it or not, I think about you a lot.

1st Radio Announcer
Your Fresno weather report coming up—

2nd Radio Announcer
Seven seventy, KKOB, Albuquerque—

Lenny
Back when you were three or four, I had a kid your age living next door, and I'd look at him and think, that's something like what you must look like. Little jeans, little Velcro tennis shoes. Riding a big wheel, making car sounds. People must have wondered why I watched him. Everywhere I lived, there was always someone I could watch.

Boy Rob
"The capital of Louisiana is Baton Rouge—"

Rob
[reading]
"All the nights searching the radio dial. All the home radio stations."

Lenny
A reasonable facsimile, as they say. I'd study 'em, and even call 'em "Robert" in my head.

Boy Rob
Ninety-one point five, KWAK, quack radio, all birds, all the time.

Rob's Grandfather
What's the difference between an accordion and an onion?

Rob's Grandmother
We give up.

Rob's Grandfather
No one cries when you chop up an accordion.

Lenny
You still there?

Rob

Yeah.

Lenny

Anyway, Rob—Jessica told me you go by "Rob." Anyway, seeing as I was out here—

Boy Rob

KOP—your station for cops and robbers. *[Sound of siren]*

Lenny

Couldn't find your mother in the book. And her folks must be unlisted. But I finally tracked down Jessica and convinced her I wasn't going to kidnap you, which I'm not. And she filled me in on things and about Rose being married, and said you'd be on the radio tonight. I really just wanted to hear your voice. But then when you gave the number it seemed crazy for us not to at least talk. At least for a minute. If you like.

Rob's Mother
[singing]
"In May I sing night and day,
In June I change my tune—"

Opera Radio Host

—she sings her famous aria, *Un bel dì*, describing in detail how he will one day sail into the harbor, come up the hill—

Lenny

Don't worry. I'm not coming over. She wouldn't even tell me where you're living. Not that I deserve to see you. 'Cause I don't. I think I'd come apart at the seams if I saw you. So the telephone is just right. Just hearing your voice is enough of a thrill.

Rob's Grandmother

"When will you pay me?
Say the bells of Old Bailey."

Lenny

It's strange to say, but it's amazing to find out how real you are. You've got a grown-up voice. I could hear the chair squeak over the air. You've got a body. You're solid. You made the chair squeak. You've got your own shadow when you're walking down the sidewalk. It's amazing.

Rob's Mother

And he knew he wasn't ready. Which he wasn't. He knew himself. I was the one who'd misjudged.

Lenny

It sounds like Rose has been great for a mother, which I knew she would be. And that her husband's a good guy. Which I'm glad for. I really am.

Mr. McCarthy
"Music, when soft voices die—"

Boy Rob
"In a Sieve they went to sea:
In spite of all their friends could say—"

Rob
[reading]
"There he was. There was my chance to ask him anything I wanted."

Rob's Mother
We were happy. We were in love. I smiled for two years. And then I got pregnant.

Aunt Jessica
You? You were positively edible, the cutest little boy on—

Lenny
Anyway, I just want you to know I think you're great. And I know I can't take any credit for that. And that it only would have been worse if I'd been around.

Rob
[reading]
"There was my chance to blast him, to tell how I'd tracked him through the airwaves, how I'd done all my

school reports on Louisiana in his honor, how I knew his face and habits and brand of accordion but that he'd never bothered to learn the first thing about me. But the words weren't waiting on my tongue, as they'd once been."

Boy Rob
Now say "Sweet dreams."

Rob's Mother
Fais de beaux rêves.

Lenny
And I don't blame you for whatever you think about me. I'm sure it's not good. And I'm sure I deserve it. But I did get to wondering what Rose told you, about her going ahead with having you on her own. Maybe you don't know it, but she—

Rob
She told me.

Rob's Mother
[singing]
"In July far, far I fly,
In August—"

Lenny
Well, good. . . . If I could have sent money to help out, I sure would have.

Aunt June
Good old Anne-Marie. I always knew when you guys were coming 'cause you could hear that car—

Lenny
Hearing you on the air gave me a feeling I don't think you'd believe. To think that you're doing radio . . . it made me think that maybe you don't actually hate every bone in my body.

Rob's Mother
I told him I was going ahead no matter what he did, that the decision and the responsibility were mine—

Lenny
Can I ask you a question?

4th Female Caller
—"I'm Gonna Wash That Man Right Outa My Hair" and I'd like you to play it really loud.

Rob
Go ahead.

Lenny
I'd just like to ask . . . do you hate me?

[long pause, the silence occupied by the calls and twitterings on the sound-effects recording]

Rob

I used to.

Lenny

What about now?

[long pause]

Rob

I don't know. It's like you're more like a stranger. Not really connected to my life. I really don't think about you anymore.

Lenny

Would you like me to be . . . more connected?

Rob

Not really.

Lenny

Not in person. I could maybe just call, just every once in a while.

Rob
[reading]

"'On the Air' should have been on his coat of arms. He was a voice without a body. An insubstantial spirit. A creature of air. A true radio man."

Lenny

Just on the telephone.

[pause]

Rob

I'm happy with my life the way it is. And the people in it.

[pause]

Lenny

That's good to hear, Rob. I'm glad for you.

3rd Radio Announcer

Drink plenty of liquids and keep your radio tuned to the coolest place on the dial—KWKH, Shreveport.

Lenny

Say. Did you get the record and the tape I left you when you were a baby?

Rob

Yeah.

Lenny

Good.

Rob's Mother
[singing]
"In August away I must."

Lenny
I always wondered about that.

Audiobook Reader
"To the tintinnabulation that so musically wells
From the bells, bells, bells—"

Lenny
Well, it's been good to hear you. It's the first time I've actually heard your voice. I've got this thing—I always remember where I was the first time I hear a piece of music. And I'm gonna remember this, believe me.

Rob
[reading]
"I almost asked him where he was, but didn't."

Lenny
I'll let you get back to business. It's pretty late. After one. Another night owl, huh?

Rob
Yeah.

Rob's Mother

Sure. The Whispering Gallery. In the dome at St. Paul's.

Lenny

Well. Time to sign off, I guess.

Rob

[reading]

"And he hung up."

[The sound-effects recording gradually fades out. There's a moment of silence before the following lines.]

Andy

You're kneeling. Arms at your sides, very loose.

Rob

[reading]

"I lay on the bed. After a minute I rolled onto the floor and got into the fallen leaf."

Andy

Now very slowly bend forward until your forehead is resting on the floor. Your arms are still at your sides, pointing behind you. Your palms are up.

Rob
[reading]

"How strange it all was. He'd felt justified in abandoning a child he'd never asked for; I'd felt righteous in my longing for his attention. All these years later, he was ready for a relationship, by which time I no longer missed him. We were riding a seesaw, facing each other up or down."

Boy Rob

What does it mean? The words are in French.

Rob's Mother

Such a beautiful song, but the words are sad. The man says he woke up in the morning and that he sat on his bed and cried.

Boy Rob

Why?

Rob's Mother

Because he had a dream about the woman he loves, who has the little black eyes. She's gone, and he knows he's never going to see her again.

Rob
[reading]

"What had brought on his call? A terminal disease? A surge of longing for a son? Guilt snowballing down the decades? An Ann Landers column? Gnawing curiosity? Why hadn't I asked him? I knew I'd seemed cold. He'd probably taken my unresponsiveness for revenge: me rejecting him with silence, payment for the sixteen years' dead air I'd received from him. But he'd forfeited my interest in him years before. After so long without an appearance, he'd slipped into the strange category of People of Indirect or Temporary Importance, joining the doctor who'd delivered me, my baby-sitters, the unseen secretary who'd typed my name on the middle-school graduation list. The old accusations felt like another character's lines. I hadn't been positive, when I'd brought the shortwave down from the attic, whether I'd actually changed or just convinced myself I had. Now I knew."

Rob's Mother
Like crossing the equator on a ship—invisible, but real. And when I'd crossed it—

Andy
Now close your eyes. Try to slow down your breathing.

Rob
[reading]
"The call had been an earthquake, an unexpected jolt. But my walls hadn't collapsed. Actually, I felt oddly calm. The fallen leaf is the most stable of shapes.

This time I felt I hadn't simply twisted my unwilling limbs into it, but that I possessed it within me."

Rob's Mother

Forgiving doesn't mean you approve of what someone did. It means you understand why they did it. Once you understand, it's easier to stop condemning and focus on the present instead—

Rob

[reading]

"November 2nd. Story idea: Divorced father, moves out of state, observes girl same age as his daughter. Gives presents. Parents alarmed, move away. He follows. Voyeur parent."

Neva

I was reading on the air, completely unaware—

Rob's Mother

I can't believe Jessica didn't prepare you.

Rob

She did. She left a message on the machine, but with everything going on to get ready for the broadcast, I didn't play it till today.

Rob's Mother

Where's he living?

Rob

I don't know.

Neva

Is he DJing?

Rob

Don't know.

Rob's Mother

Is he married?

Rob

Didn't ask.

Rob's Mother

I wish I'd been here.

Rob

Actually, you were. In the Whispering Gallery.

[We hear the sound-effects recording. It begins fading out after half a minute, overlapping the following speech.]

Lenny

—*my last show here at "The Ghost Raising," so I'm gonna go out with my own request. Which I want to dedicate to a new listener. One of our youngest listeners out there. A listener named Robert Allan Radkovitz, pretty newly*

arrived in the world, a precious member of our radio family.
Robert, this sweet Cajun waltz is for you, the same way it
was for your mother. And from what I hear, you've got the
looks that fit it, so here it is—"Little Black Eyes."

[We hear the beginning of "Little Black Eyes." After half a
minute, it begins fading out, overlapping the following
speech.]

Rob
[reading]
"It's been six months since the call. Life, as I'd told
Lenny, is quite sufficiently full and fulfilling. I've had
some terrific teachers this year who've—"

Neva
Discreet, Rob. Very smooth. No doubt McCarthy
will never notice this *flagrant attempt at bribery.*

Rob
[reading]
"We're still doing broadcasts on KPOW. I'm working
on a short story I want to read at the next writers'
group meeting."

Neva
How about, "Neva and I are even more madly in
love and are currently reading an anthology of erotic
stories"?

Rob
Do you really think he needs to know that?

Neva
Could help him keep turning the pages.

Rob
[reading]
"There hasn't been any further word from Lenny. On my part, there's been more understanding, and more recognition of how lucky I've been with the family that raised me. I'm—"

Rob's Grandmother
I'd love it. You're a dear, Robbie. The Agatha Christie, on the dresser. There's a bookmark. I like your voice so much better than the ones on the tapes.

Rob
[reading]
"January 8th. Realizing how scared Lenny must have been. Realizing when I was conceived, Lenny was only eight years older than I am now. Were a girl-friend of mine to get pregnant against my wishes and vow to raise the child by herself, would the child have lifetime claim on me? Strangeness of standing in both our shoes."

Neva
"Your little voice over the wires came leaping—"

Rob
[reading]
"I also find myself wondering about the answers to all the questions I never asked him. I have no way to contact him—this time, by my own doing. I wonder if he'll seek me out in the future. It wouldn't surprise me, since he has the number. Halloween, when the spirits return to earth for one night, comes around every year."

Lenny
You know what trick-or-treating's really about? Making the dead one's favorite foods. That's what brings 'em back home.

Rob
[reading]
"Perhaps, some year, I'll even make gumbo."

[The sound-effects recording comes up, then gradually fades out.]

THE END

Performance Notes

Though there are fifty-two characters in *Seek*, a reader's theater performance could be brought off by as few as fifteen speakers, with nine taking the main roles and six playing multiple, minor roles. A radio play or stage adaptation might require more speakers to aid the audience in identifying voices. A few further remarks:

If the gender of a role isn't obvious, a reader of either sex can read it. In the case of the radio announcers, who often give their own first names, feel free to change those names to match the gender of the reader. The baseball announcers should be male.

The melody of the lullaby sung by Rob's mother can be improvised. The composer Benjamin Britten wrote a hauntingly wistful tune for the words that could also be used; it appears in his collection *Friday Afternoons*.

"Little Black Eyes" is a popular Cajun song, sometimes known as "Little Dark Eyes" or more commonly by its French title "'Tits Yeux Noirs." It's been recorded by nearly every Cajun group.

The performer reading the part of Rob's mother needs to be able to pronounce French and Spanish. Those reading the Spanish TV Actor and Actress and the Spanish DJ need to be able to pronounce Spanish.

For public performance rights, please contact Permissions Manager, Cricket Books, 315 Fifth Street, Peru, Illinois 61354.

Cast

In order of appearance

Major Roles

Rob
Rob's Mother
Rob's Grandmother
Rob's Grandfather
Aunt June
Boy Rob
Lenny
Aunt Jessica
Zad

Minor Roles

Opera Radio Host
1st Radio Announcer
Spanish TV Actress
Mr. McCarthy
2nd Radio Announcer
1st Female Caller
Exercise Video Voice
Audiobook Reader
Spanish TV Actor
Female Writer
Male Writer
Mrs. Kathos
2nd Female Caller
Teacher

Nick
Woman on Telephone
3rd Radio Announcer
Radio Psychic
Psychic Show Caller
Spanish DJ
4th Radio Announcer
5th Radio Announcer
1st Male Caller
2nd Male Caller
Ray
3rd Female Caller
1st Student
2nd Student
3rd Student
4th Student
Female English Teacher
Coach
Dean
Mrs. Druckenmuller
Sports Editor
Penelope
Andy
Tango Teacher
4th Female Caller
3rd Male Caller
Neva
James
Old Man